Purrfectly Naughty

A MAVERICK PRIDE TALE

THE MAVERICK PRIDE TALES
BOOK FIVE

C.D. GORRI

Purrfectly Naughty:
A Maverick Pride Tale 5
by C.D. Gorri
Edited by BookNookNuts

Copyright 2022 C.D. Gorri

Happy Holidays and thanks for Joining the Maverick Pride!
I hope you are enjoying this purrfectly awesome tales as much as I am.
And remember, naughty or nice, you're always on someone's list!

Before you begin sign up for my newsletter here.

Sometimes being naughty is very, very nice...

Pamela has turned her life around for the sake of her son and the Maverick Pride, but is this reformed bad girl ready for more than one night of naughtiness?

Her main focus is to provide her cub with the best life possible. She's worked hard to mend her past mistakes, earning a second chance to make a good life for Paulie and herself. Forging relationships with her Pride mates is no small feat, but totally worth it to this she-Cat. Especially when the Nari chooses her to represent the entire Pride at Uncle Uzzi's *Magical Holiday Ball.*

Javier Auberon is an Andean Bear Shifter who's recently moved to the states from his South American home. Spending the holidays with his favorite honorary uncle, the owner of the renowned *Uncle Uzzi's Magical Matchmaking Service*—Uncle Uzzi himself—is a no-brainer.

Uncle Uzzi has been trying to find a match for Javi through his services forever, but the Bear had no idea he'd meet his fated mate at the old Witch's famous holiday party. She's in denial, but he's not giving up.

Can Javi make all of Pamela's Christmas wishes come true?

You are invited to Uncle Uzzi's Magical Holiday Ball!

Seasons Greetings!

You are cordially invited to celebrate this holiday season with Uncle Uzzi at his Evergreen Estate for a Magical Holiday Ball!

All of the guests are affiliated somehow with Uncle Uzzi's Magical Matchmaking Service, so do not worry, my dears, you will be with good company. This is a time to be thankful for our blessings and to feel joyful for having one another.

Thank you.

P.S.
As in previous years, charitable donations are being
collected in the main ballroom, contact my assistant
Bernice for more information.

Prologue

Uncle Uzzi picked up the box of addressed invitations and ran his ringed hand over the silver embossed envelopes before stopping on a seemingly random one.

He still wore his wedding ring, the simple gold band as beloved now as when his liebling had placed it on his finger. It was the same finger he used for scrying, a necessary tool of his trade. The owner and operator of *Uncle Uzzi's Magical Matchmaking Service,* he'd made many a match with that finger.

Satisfaction filled him as he thought of all the happy couples, triads, and fated mates he had placed together over the years. His success was only measured by the happiness of his clients, and now he would get the chance to see some of them again.

It was the holiday season, Uzzi's favorite time of year. Every yuletide he organized a ball, collecting charitable contributions to distribute to the less fortunate was a way his couples paid it forward, a tradition started by his sweet Betty. He felt her spirit fill him as he ran his hand over the top of that pesky little envelope that had caught his attention.

Hmmm. Can it be true? Is it time?

He tapped the invitation one more time, trailing over the rest of them to see if it was merely static electricity or something. But no, he knew better than that. Even after three tries, he just kept coming back to that one particular invite over and over again.

Must be time for certain.

Shivers tickled his spine and a small mischievous grin played at the corner of his mouth. Uzzi pulled the envelope out from the pile. *Ah yes,* he thought to himself, his magic pulsing wildly—the innate powers he'd been blessed with, passed on by the Goddess of Love herself, were practically sizzling in approval.

This one was special.

Uncle Uzzi looked at the name and address and a bark of laughter escaped his lips. This was going to be wonderful.

"Oh, Javi, it has been too long," he said to no one

in particular. "I have a feeling this is going to be the most memorable Christmas of your life, *osito*."

Uncle Uzzi used the special nickname his beloved wife used to call her favorite nephew. He'd watched this Shifter grow up and had been calling Javier Auberon *osito* or *little Bear* in his native Spanish ever since he was a cub.

It was an old joke, one he'd probably outgrown. But, oh well. He was an old Witch now, and the young could always afford the old some patience and indulgence. Besides, big Bear or not, Uzzi could still zap him with a spell if he got growly about it.

Ha ha ha. Or was it ho ho ho?

He laughed at his own joke placing the envelope on top of his pile. Seriously though, Javi was one of Uzzi's favorite honorary nephews. The younger son of one of his beloved *liebling's* oldest and dearest friends. Together, they had watched Javi and his brother grow. And now, it seemed, he would watch him find his mate.

"You see, *liebling*," he murmured to his wife, speaking aloud as he often did to her. "Your little *osito* will be just fine."

Uncle Uzzi was a sucker for happy holiday endings, *or beginnings,* as it were. This was no different a start to a hundred other happy ever afters he had been fortunate enough to be part of, and yet, it was special.

It was the holiday season, after all. And whether it was Christmas, Hannukah, Solstice, Kwanzaa, or another feast that was honored and remembered, the point was—this was a time for celebrating life, and what better way than to fall in love?

When was the last time Uzzi had spoken to his nephew, anyway? Ah yes, that handsome Bear had written to him earlier that month to inform Uzzi of his coming to the area around this time.

Purrfect, Uzzi thought, and there it was. That sudden inspirational zing that told him he was about to make a match. And with his favorite Pride, too.

How exciting!

It seemed *osito* was moving to the states for good. So, naturally, Uzzi had made sure to include him on the invitation list for the holiday party. Of course, his special little insight hadn't kicked in until just now, but he understood. Magic worked in mysterious ways.

"What a surprise you are in for, *osito*," he whispered, nodding approvingly.

This year, little Javi was going to get a present he would never forget. Uncle Uzzi hummed Christmas Carols as he walked down to the car and handed the driver the box of invitations to be mailed.

"Good morning, Hank," Uzzi said, and smiled at the Shifter whose car services he often used whenever he traveled to Maverick Point to visit a certain Tiger Pride.

"Hello, Uncle Uzzi. Ready to head to Maverick Point?"

"Indeed, I am. But let's drop by Barvale for some treats on the way, yes? The twins did love those Strawberry Bear Claws I sent last month."

"Of course," Hank replied easily.

Good man. He really needed a mate though. Hmmm.

Uzzi would think on that, later perhaps. He was sending a text to Elissa to let her know his change of plans. He was supposed to drop off a gift for the Nari and Neta's six-month old twin daughters, Melly, and Celia, but Uzzi had another mission now.

A very special mission to deliver an invitation to his very special *Magical Holiday Ball* to a very special person.

Uncle Uzzi clapped his hands in anticipation as Hank turned onto the highway that would lead to the Maverick Point and then to the Pride House.

He was practically vibrating with glee at the thought of delivering a *happy ever after* to one of his favorite people. Pamela Brown had a tough beginning—that was an understatement. But she was working so hard and doing so well now. The she-Tiger was Uzzi's favorite redemption story.

Pamela was due for a happy ending, and with a little bit of luck, and some magic, her year would end with a bang! A peal of laughter escaped his lips, and he noted Hank's quirked brows as he glanced in the rearview mirror.

"Everything alright, Uncle Uzzi?"

"Oh, Hank, I really think it will be," he said, and glanced out the window at the wintry scenery rushing by.

"Another feeling then, eh, Uncle Uzzi?"

"Indeed, Hank. I believe everything is going to be *purrfect* for a certain couple this holiday season."

Chapter One

"What do you mean, I'm going to a ball? Do I look like *Cinderella?*" Pamela Brown raised one eyebrow at her unusually perky Nari and glanced down at the precious pink-cheeked baby she was holding.

Pam loved babies. She'd spent so much of Paulie's infancy trying to keep him safe, it seemed so far away now. Getting cuddle time with little Celia and Melly was her favorite time of day.

She loved those twins to pieces and was honored when the Nari had insisted that Pamela allow them to call her *Aunt Pam*. The memory still brought tears to her eyes. She couldn't wait to spoil the little princesses when they were old enough. Even her son was enamored of the twins.

"Auntie Pammy-wammy is gonna get dwessed up weal pwetty and go to a dancy-wancy, yes, she is," Elissa cooed and babbled to the infant she was currently dressing, and this time, both Pamela's eyebrows went sky high.

Ookaayy.

Something was definitely up with the tiny blonde woman Pamela had grown to trust and love over the past year since she'd mated the Pride Neta. Elissa had been born a normal, but once she'd received the mating bite, she'd experienced the *Puspa*.

Now a powerful white Tiger and the Nari of the Maverick Pride, Elissa ruled by her mate's side, and earned the love and respect of everyone in the Pride. Pamela included.

The rare gift of the Puspa, or the *Change*, had been bestowed upon the Alpha couple by the Fates themselves—doubly blessing her mating to Hunter Maverick in a way that was unheard of these days. Their love story was the stuff fairytales and legends were made of.

If only.

Pamela acknowledged their fabulous love story with a wistful sigh. She had never known that kind of singular devotion, and probably never would.

Lucky them.

But it was more than luck. It was Fate. Truth was, Pamela did not know anyone more deserving of a *happy ever after* than the Neta and Nari. She couldn't be happier for the two of them. Their love and powerful matebond were testaments to the strength of the Pride.

A Pride Pamela had once undercut with her mistaken loyalty to the former, and now thankfully deceased, Beta, Blake Segal. Her she-Cat paced at the unhappy reminder, and she closed her eyes to soothe the beast.

He is gone now. Can't hurt us anymore. Grrr.

Blake had been bad news from the start, but using his innate charm and charisma, he'd managed to fool her, and others in the Pride. He'd caused untold damage to the infrastructure of the Maverick Pride, hurt so many of the males and females he should have been protecting. And then there was Paulie. Ignoring her son was the best thing that sonovabitch had ever done.

At least now, the Pride bonds were being slowly mended through the efforts of Hunter, Elissa, the Tigers of the Honor Guard, and their mates. And in a small way, even by Pamela herself. She was trying to correct the wrongs she'd done in every way possible. Especially since that meant a better life for her precious cub.

Happy and grateful for the chance, Pamela was doing things she never thought possible. She was making connections and friends with the women of the Pride whom she'd once viewed as enemies. Blake had poisoned her mind and set her against the others, filling her head with lies and abusing her trust and self-esteem until it had been nonexistent.

But that was in the past. Pamela was moving on with her life. She was trying, but still, she had no expectations about her position in the Pride. She was just damn grateful they had not thrown her out. Cue her being positively stunned by Elissa's surprising news.

"Are you gonna make me get official, Pam?" the Naris asked, squinting her eyes. "Fine. Pamela Brown, I want you to go to Uncle Uzzi's party as a representative of the Pride."

"What? No way, you don't want me to do that, Liss," Pamela said, rocking the baby too quickly and earning that tug in her hair from the infant. "Sorry, *bugaboo*," she murmured kissing the babe's sweet head.

"Yes, way, and the baby is fine. She's a Tiger cub, a little rocking won't hurt her—now where was I?

Oh yeah, you are going to go. You'll drink, eat, dance, have fun!"

"You should go with Hunter—"

"Nope. Not happening. Come on, Pam. Please? I don't want to leave the babies and it will be too noisy for them. And everyone else is pregnant," she snorted.

"Yeah, that's true. Your friends are super easy," Pam joked, then raised her eyes to Elissa's uncertain about her lame joke.

"OMG! That is a good one. I am so stealing that and using it on Jess." She smirked.

Whew! That was close.

"Look, Liss, I'm sorry but I can't represent the Pride, I–"

"Yes, you can, Pamela. Don't make me use my Nari voice on you."

"You're serious, aren't you?"

"As a heart attack. Alright? You good? Yes!"

Finally, Pamela nodded, caving in, even though it made her nervous as hell. Imagine her representing the Pride at one of the infamous get togethers hosted by none other than Uncle Uzzi himself. The older matchmaking Witch was well-known and respected in Shifter circles, especially in Maverick Point.

Oh gods. What was she going to wear? Who was she going to talk to? This was a bad idea.

Pamela turned to tell the Nari, but then Elissa was on the plush baby mat on the floor, talking baby talk about Pamela's upcoming night out.

"Aunt Pammy Wammy is gonna get some yummy num-nums. Yes, that's right. It's time she got her musty, old stocking stuffed—yes, she is!"

"OMG! Lissa! First, it's not that old or musty—you know what? I think you've been around dirty diapers all day, Liss," she snapped at her friend and Nari, who was now giggling hysterically. "Seriously, woman. Maybe the fumes are getting to you?"

The Nari answered by keeling over in a fit of giggles and snorting. Loudly.

Pam was so fucked. There was no way she was getting out of this.

Shit shit shit.

"No, I have not been sniffing too many baby bottoms today, Miss Brown. You just make sure Marion has time to wax you before you get ready for the ball, *Pamerella*. That man is a genius with the wand," Elissa informed her.

She leaned over to blow a raspberry on her other daughter's tummy, tying her little pink shoelace before reaching out to swap babies with Pamela.

"Hunter doesn't get mad when Marion waxes you?"

"Hell, yeah, he does. My sexy shaved Neta gets mad with passion, that is. My mate can't stand the scent of another man anywhere near me, even when he knows it's platonic. Just makes him want to claim what he already knows is his."

"Is that why you started waxing twice a month when we both know you don't need it?"

"Yep!"

Elissa held her fist in the air for a bump, and Pamela indulged her, reluctantly. This was a conversation she did not want to touch with a ten-foot pole.

Imagine—that little blonde female was knowingly goading an Alpha male Shifter, one as powerful as the Neta, but having her girly bits waxed by another male—a gay male. But still, a male.

Damn, Pamela had to give it up to Elissa. She had to admire the brass ovaries on that woman.

Holy shit. The Nari is a motherfucking badass.

"Alright, I think she's ready," Elissa pursed her lips at her daughter, and Pamela smiled at the gorgeous baby's Christmas splendor.

Today the Nari was hosting a *photos-with-Santa* event at the Pride House for all the cubs and her daughters looked like little pink presents with pretty velvet bows tied around their tummies. Pamela had volunteered to help for the event, and somehow, she wound up dressed as a Christmas Elf of all things.

Her inner she-Tiger chuffed in annoyance at the silly red and green sequins and the white faux-fur trim that made up the costume, but Pamela loved Christmas, and she was more than game.

She carried one precious infant while the Nari held the other and waited patiently for Elissa to finish explaining her nutty idea.

A holiday ball? Her? What would she even wear to something like that?

The Nari was clearly not thinking straight. Then again, things always went a little sideways when Uncle Uzzi came to visit, and she'd seen the Witch's car in the driveway when she'd arrived. Maybe that was why Elissa was still a little bit giddy.

"Did you see the lights Hunter and Brayden put up outside?" Elissa asked, and Pamela smiled and nodded while she chatted about the Christmas decorations.

Yes, Pam had noticed. The Pride House looked incredible, but the she-Cat was a little preoccupied at the moment. Fear and shame welled up inside of her at the thought of doing anything to embarrass them, her people—*the Maverick Pride*, at the event. What if she messed it up so badly, they hated her and wanted her to leave? Fear gripped her heart as she looked at the faces of those she had grown to rely on.

Until about a year ago, things were very different for Pamela. She'd been used and manipulated, passed around among Blake and his Shifter friends like some sort of possession. How could she have been so stupid? The truth was, she thought she loved Blake. After all, he'd given her Paulie.

The sounds of her now six-year-old cub running through the Pride House, giggling away, reached her sensitive ears and Pamela said a small prayer to whoever listened that her young stayed happy and safe.

He was a different boy now that she had earned a place for them there. Her work with the *Maverick Pride Support Group*, led by Gretchen and Reg Cray, had done wonders for her self-confidence. It also helped erase those mistakes from her past.

Still, she bit her lip and wondered. Was she worthy to represent them at Uncle Uzzi's holiday bash? She wasn't so sure.

"Liss, I don't think I can go to that party," she explained.

"Pamela, you were born into this Pride," Elissa interrupted her negative thoughts. "Who could better represent us? Uncle Uzzi has asked for you, personally, and after all he has done for us, it would be insulting not to attend," she finished, and Pamela had to agree with her words.

"I have nothing to wear," she used her last and best excuse to try to sway her friend, but the maddening woman simply laughed.

"Like that is a problem! Um, hello, Nari here whose sis-in-law has a boutique in town. Duh!" she said and snorted. Pamela just laughed.

She used to be quite the fashion disaster, but once she'd stopped allowing herself to be Blake's victim, she threw away all her notions of what was sexy and attractive. That had been his doing—the makeup, hair, and the too tight clothes. She had starved herself to be skinny enough for him. Had bleached her curly hair and wore the slinkiest little designer outfits to please him.

Grrr.

Pamela was quite unrecognizable now. She'd gained at least twenty-five pounds of weight this past year, grew the bleach out of her hair, and had it cut. And best of all, she often wore only comfortable jeans or yoga pants with big billowy tops.

After all, her job as one of the only two manicurists, plus her promotion to junior hairstylist at Gretchen's salon, did not require heels and couture.

But a Christmas ball certainly would. Sigh.

"I am so honored you asked me, but Liss, I can't afford to spend money on a gown. It's Christmas and I am getting Paulie that bike he wants if it kills me."

"Girl, do you think I'd let you go somewhere looking like a pauper? Look, Jessica is bringing over some selections from her shop this afternoon and you are gonna love them, and best of all, it will be free publicity for her. Just think how many of Uncle Uzzi's guests will like it, and they might ask where you got it," Elissa said excitedly.

"Really? That is so nice, especially with her being in her third trimester," Pamela replied and inhaled deeply, trying not to give into tears.

It still moved her to think how kind all the women had been to her ever since the truth about her situation had come out. She'd been really awful to Jessica, Gretchen, Kylie, and Elissa too, back when she'd first met them.

Mostly, she'd been horrible to Gretchen. No number of apologies could make up for what she'd done, but the wonderful woman had not only hired her, but she'd welcomed her into her closest circle of friends.

Pamela worked hard to make it up to them. She would do anything to repair the damage she'd done because of her own warped image of herself and females in general as a result of Blake's abuse and lies. In fact, she'd thrown herself into the support group Gretchen was kind enough to host. Now, she was finally in a good place, both mentally and physically. The only thing left was to try to make the best life she could for Paulie.

It was difficult for her to trust anyone around him, after all, he was the offspring of the man who'd done nothing but hurt the Pride, but Hunter Maverick was not the average Neta.

He had really surprised her. He was a forgiving and nonjudgmental man who'd welcomed Paulie with open arms and assured Pamela it was what any good leader would do.

Yes, this Christmas was going to be good for them both.

Chapter Two

Maverick Point was the only place Pamela had ever lived, and it was the only place she wanted to live. Being asked to go to the ball to represent the Pride was like a dream. Her inner she-Tiger chuffed in agreement.

Her relationship with her she-Cat had grown stronger with her self-healing and the work she'd been doing to repair the damage Blake had done to her psyche. She was doing well now.

It seemed Blake's treatment of her had hurt parts of her, making her feel like an outsider in her own Pride. Pamela wanted to belong, for her sake and Paulie's. She did, and now she finally knew it, and that was what mattered.

"Nice of Jess? My ass!" Elissa said aloud, disrupting Pam's train of thought.

Christmas carols and the sounds of folks talking and children laughing rang out from all over the Pride House. Jessica was Elissa's sister-in-law and something of a sass-master, so she understood her comment.

Pamela liked Jess, sass, and all. She followed behind Liss, who was chatting about the heavily pregnant redhead, and the gift she and Hunter were giving her for the baby, as they walked through the hallway. Elissa sure was funny, but Pamela hid her smile behind the baby in her arms.

"She's big as a house and cranky as hell, waiting for that Bear cub of hers to come popping out."

"Could be a Tiger," Pamela said, and it was true. No one knew which Shifter genes would be dominant when two different species had young together.

"For her sake, I hope it's a boy, cause she is already bigger than I was with two," she grinned wickedly. "And her temper has been way off balance. Lucky beyotch. Only a man can do that to a woman," Elissa said, nodding sagely. "Even little men in utero."

Pamela snorted. It was true, Jessica had been behaving a teensy weensy—okay, a whole freaking lot—like her Black Bear mate. Especially since she hit her third trimester. It was so cute watching Brayden, their big, burly Beta go to pieces when he came in the other day holding an image of the latest ultrasound image. It was a weird grainy blob, but he acted like he was looking at the Mona Lisa.

To him, he was, she supposed. Jess was stretched to the max, cried at the drop of a hat, went into a murderous rage if anyone ate the cookie dough before she got to it, and her ankles were so swollen she no longer wore shoes, but Pam envied her. She envied all of them—but with only the best intentions, of course.

Heck, it seemed everyone was either pregnant or taking care of new cubs just lately. It was enough to give a gal baby fever.

Sigh.

Chuff.

Purrrrrrrrrrrrrrrrrr.

Lucky for Pamela, she'd had her cub young, and he was the best of the best—in her *not so humble* opinion. A smile spread across her face as she thought about her baby boy. Paulie was already in the middle of kindergarten, but he would always be her sweet cub.

He was still into cuddles and kisses, thank goodness, but she missed him being a baby. She was a different person then, and the joy and pleasure of being a mother had been muted in her need for secrecy.

It had taken a lot of effort to keep his birth a secret, always hiding him away from the rest of the Pride. Blake hadn't wanted a cub. And she sure as hell did not want anyone to know she was its mother. Like a dirty secret, he'd pushed her aside, denied Paulie's existence, but still she stayed.

Her esteem had taken such a beating, Pamela did not believe she deserved any better. She'd been little more than a thrall—a lovesick, mindless servant where the evil ex-Beta was concerned.

Shame welled inside of her at what she'd allowed from that creep. The things she had put up with. The humiliating treatment she'd been subjected to. It always amazed her how the smallest hint of pride or pleasure from him had made her esteem soar, but the slightest snarl or disapproval used to send her spiraling.

Too many good people allowed others to dictate how they felt, and that was not okay. Her work with the support group focused on self-love and healthy self-images. It was important work—necessary work for someone like her.

Pamela was different now. She was not a love-starved girl looking for a father figure to make her whole anymore. She was a Tiger. A fierce, powerful woman who did not need a man to be complete.

She was a single mother who loved her cub and had an important role in her Pride. A she-Cat who took pleasure in contributing to the good of her community. She was not the Pamela Brown she used to be. She was better now—stronger, too. Pam just had to remember that and keep on going.

"Elissa," Hunter stalked towards them and greeted his mate with a kiss on the lips that made Pamela blush.

It was so intimate and loving. The connection between the Neta and Nari was so strong it was almost tangible. Pamela certainly felt it in the Pride bonds, and it gave her a sense of peace, something her inner animal longed for. Their commitment to each other was a force to be reckoned with.

"Hunter," the Nari returned, and smiled up at her mate.

Pamela figured they'd need a moment alone, so she stepped forward and handed the cub she'd been holding to Hunter's outstretched arms. He was as good a father as he was a leader, and she was glad that he had found happiness.

"Excuse me, I have to go tend to my duties," she said with a silly curtsey in her Elf costume. "Oh, and Elissa, I would be proud to represent our Pride at the ball," Pamela added before leaving the Alpha family alone.

The bells on her shoes jingled as she headed over to where Brayden was sitting in a large, velvet lined chair dressed like Santa Claus. The Bear Shifter did not look happy, but in her honest opinion, he was the best possible choice for Santa. No one else was quite as big, though he did have to stuff his jacket with a pillow, or so she thought. The beard was definitely fake—but the tummy, who knew?

"No fat jokes," Brayden grumbled, and Pamela laughed as a couple of dozen unruly cubs came running into the room where they were still setting up.

"Hey everyone," Pierce, another of the Neta's guards, called out. "We are going to take our pictures in just a minute, but Santa needs all of you to be good little cubs, so listen to his helper, Miss Elf, while you wait your turn and maybe you'll get a present for your efforts!" Pierce grinned widely and winked at Pamela, who curtsied to the children.

She started the music—a fun sing-along track with carols the kids all knew. Next, she organized the cubs into a line. They were so adorable, dressed up in their holiday best and jumping up and down excitedly while she handed out candy canes and little gifts to keep the energetic cuties occupied.

Pierce was acting as the photographer, and another Honor guard, Lance, was there to lend a hand as well. They had just under thirty of the Pride's children present, and she knew she was in for a long day. Paulie waved at her from his spot in line next to his two best friends, and her heart squeezed. He was so precious to her, and this was the first Christmas she had ever seen him so excited.

"Hi Mama—I mean Miss Elf," he said, giggling wildly.

"Hello to you, have you all been good cubs?" she asked him and his friends, letting them pick from her bag of treats.

"Okay, boys and girls, let's sing Hark the Herald!"

Chapter Three

What a wonderful time!

Hours later, Pamela took off her pointy hat and fake elf ears with a relieved sigh. She tossed them over at Elissa, who was sitting at the kitchen table with Jessica. A couple of mugs of steaming hot cocoa sat between them.

"Hey! Ooh, I always wanted a pair of these. Wonder if Hunter will be into some boudoir cosplay," she said with a waggle of her eyebrows.

"TMI, Nari. Really, that is TMI," Pamela replied with a shake of her head.

"Sit down, Miss Elf, you had a hard day," Jessica said and handed her a mug.

Mmm.

"What are the chances this one is spiked?" Pamela asked, and sighed wistfully. She could definitely use a little *rum pum pum pum* in her hot cocoa.

"I don't know if you earned any of this special rum straight from Puerto Rico Uncle Uzzi brought me," Elissa teased, pulling a bottle of the delicious gold goodness out from under the table.

"No fair, guys. I can't drink," Jessica whined.

"Oh hush. You're growing a football team in that stomach of yours, you can drink after," Elissa told her.

"Look, I love you both, but Elissa, you owe me at least one shot in my cocoa after little Nancy got nervous and barfed candy cane all over my Elf shoes. I had to borrow Pierce's flip flops and they are four sizes too big," she groaned and sank into one of the chairs looking down at her bell-less toes.

"Awwww. Yeah, that did suck. Okay, here ya go. So, did everything go okay? I had to get the twins down for a nap, so I am afraid I missed most of the event," Elissa explained.

"It went really well, actually, and I mean that, Liss. Paulie had a great time. He's helping Pierce and Lance clean up, then they are taking him for a burger," she said, not bothering to hide her grin. She was so stinking proud of her little cub.

"That's great! That means we can try on the dresses I brought." Jessica grinned ruefully and patted her large tummy, before she added, "Well, you can try them on, and I will be the judge!"

"Thank you, Jess. I really don't know about this, I mean, I put on some weight since the last time I got dressed up. Maybe I should crash diet. When is the party, anyway?"

"Tomorrow night, and no, you look gorgeous. Really, I mean, who even knew you had tits before? You were so damn skinny, but now, *kapow*, it'll be watchout sexy Santas!" Elissa yelled and waggled her eyebrows.

"Lissa," she groaned her name, snorting as she tried to hold in her laughter. "Fine, I guess I do have breasts now. But sexy Santas?"

"What's wrong with Sexy Santas? I told Brayden to bring home the hat. Mama wants to play," Jess said, stuffing an entire gingerbread bear into her mouth.

"You gals are so gross," Pamela said, shielding her eyes from the images they conjured.

"Look, *Little Miss Purity*, I have it all worked out. You are going to leave Paulie here with us, and we are gonna make popcorn and watch an animated Christmas movie. I have decided to host a Pride sleepover, and I invited little Nicholas from his class, and Steven too."

"You did?" Pam asked, disbelief clouding her eyes.

"Sure. We don't have like a traditional *Cub Scouts* or anything in Maverick Point, but I talked to Hunter, and he agrees, we should initiate a sort of club for the children of the Pride," the Nari explained. "They shouldn't be on the outside of things until they have their first shifts. We think they should develop strong community bonds with the Pride as early as possible. What do you all think?"

"I think that's a wonderful idea," Jessica agreed, and Pamela nodded her head.

She was too choked up for words and sniffed to cover up the tears that threatened to fall from her eyes. It was exactly the kind of thing Paulie needed. Her apartment was too cramped for sleepovers, and many of the moms from school were not exactly fond of Pamela.

If only the Pride had done something like that when she'd been younger. So many mistakes, so much regret, but not for her cub. He would be raised better.

Tigers were loaners in the wild, and, even though Shifters lived in groups, Tiger Prides typically had smaller numbers than most Packs or Clans. Children were often cast aside until it was known whether they could actually change into their animals. Sometimes, it was too late by then. Those same neglected children turned to gangs and bad crowds for support.

Pamela's parents had both died before she'd reached puberty, the age when Tigers typically come into their fur, and she'd had to go through it alone. She'd had no one to depend on except for an older uncle who was neglectful, to say the least.

No wonder she wound up under the thumb of a master manipulator like Blake. When Hunter had returned from college with him by his side, young Pamela had been smitten with the dangerous Shifter from Washington.

She had no idea what kind of monster lurked beneath his pristine smile. Not even after he'd ordered her to sleep with a Hyena Shifter from a neighboring Pack of the cold-hearted animals. The memory of his order still filled her with revulsion and the beating she had received when she'd refused to be used like a whore was nothing compared to the one the Hyena Shifter had given her that night Gretchen had come upon them in the park. Thank fuck she'd been found before anything truly terrible had transpired.

The Hyena had waylaid her by her car after she'd picked up work, tending bar outside of town. He'd knocked her out and brought her to the park. By the time she'd come to, Pamela's clothes had been torn to shreds, and she'd been covered in bites and scratches. Gretchen and Reg had saved her from a much worse fate.

Yes, she owed this Pride for so much. She was glad Blake was dead—happy her tormentor was gone for good. Her she-Tiger was happy too, though she would have preferred to be the one who ended his miserable life. Now, she and Paulie were safe, and her son had the chance to be happy.

"Hey, where'd you go?" Elissa asked, and Pamela blinked slowly.

"Sorry," she said. "I was just thinking."

"Thinking of the past? Well, fuck that shit," the Nari growled. "Pamela, you listen to me, none of that asshole's crap matters anymore. You are a wonderful mother and a great friend. You are a valuable member of this Pride. Now, are you ready to get gorgeous?"

"Oh, crap. Um, yeah, I guess," she said, wincing as Elissa tapped the screen of her cell phone with one red and white painted nail.

She turned on some Christmas rock music and

Gretchen and Kylie came filing into the kitchen with bags from *Jessica's Closet*.

"Look what we brought!"

"Holy cow! Panties too?"

"Of course," Kylie said, and winked.

The woman made the best lingerie Pamela had ever tried, but she was not exactly in the market for any at the moment. Still, it did not hurt to be prepared, she thought with a naughty grin.

They started unveiling the treasures they'd brought from the store and Pamela was overwhelmed at the selection. The boutique specialized in plus-sized women's clothing, and where a year ago Pamela was skinny as a twig, she'd put on some pounds in all the right areas to warrant an upgrade in sizes.

"*OHMYGAWD!*" Elissa gasped as they showed dress after spectacular dress.

"These are so beautiful, but I can't afford—"

"Nonsense. This is for the Pride, and we will bear the expense," Elissa said, and grabbed the price tag off one gown before shoving it at her. "Now, go try that on, and don't make me use my Nari voice!" she threatened playfully for the second time in so many hours.

"Okay, okay," Pamela grumbled and took the lovely confection.

She went into the bathroom and took her time dressing. She could hardly believe the results. Pamela gasped as she spun around in front of the floor-length mirror, not recognizing herself.

"Pamela? Come out already!" Elissa knocked on the door.

"Sorry," she said, and stepped out to wolf whistles from all the gathered females and their mates who happened to have joined them in the kitchen.

"Wow, Pamela. You look lovely," Hunter said and smiled kindly at her.

"Lovely? She looks completely fuckable in that dress," Jessica said. "I mean, *dayum*—I would do her."

"Jess!" Elissa yelled.

"What? Fine, I like eggplant, not tacos, but still, I don't think my tits ever looked that good. Brayden, what do you think? I mean, you seem to like them now, even though they're like baby watermelons, but I miss them being perky," Jessica rambled, and started tearing up. "Some lucky guy is gonna see Pam in that and he will get his little *freaky-fun-naughty-time* on with those two fun bags—all he has to do is just tug on the straps—then BAM, it will be on, and I can't see my feeeeeeeeeeeeeeet!" she wailed, and Brayden just looked around panicked.

The big Bear stood up and picked up his mate, princess style, kissing her head while she cried her heart out.

"Okay, I better get her home. She's a little hormonal," he shrugged, though his cheeks burned bright pink.

The big man carried his pregnant mate out to his car despite her crying, and Pamela was pretty sure she heard him say something about him always wanting to play with her fun bags—*again with the TMI.*

Pamela and the rest of the Shifters pretended they did not just hear that. Even when Jessica asked him if he liked her pregnant and Brayden answered by describing—*in terrific detail*—just how pretty her enormous bosoms were to him and what his plans were for them when he got her home. If Pam wasn't mistaken, there was bound to be a run on caramel sauce at the local market.

Eeek.

"Okay then," Elissa said and giggled. "It's all set. You are wearing that dress, and we are watching Paulie tomorrow night. And Pamela?"

"Yes, Nari," she said, returning to the bathroom

to carefully remove the dress before packing it along with accessories back in the bag.

"Remember Santa, *and Uncle Uzzi,* will be watching."

"I gotcha, I'll be nice—"

"Nice? Ew! You better be naughty!"

"Are you sure you don't mean—"

"Hell no! Naughty is the new nice," Elissa said and winked.

Pamela blushed scarlet while she gathered up her things and called for Paulie. It was definitely time to leave, but the Nari's parting words stuck in her head as she drove to her apartment to the sounds of Paulie singing carols in the back seat.

Pamela Brown hadn't been naughty in a very long time.

Maybe too long. Grrr.

Chapter Four

Javier Auberon stepped out of his gunmetal gray Mercedes G63 and deftly avoided patches of ice and snow, making it through to the immaculately shoveled brick walkway that led to one of Uncle Uzzi's many incredible mansions.

The old Witch had a dozen, as far as Javi knew. A smile played at the corner of his mouth as he adjusted the rectangular wooden box tucked in his arm. A limited edition of the man's favorite label made by a vintner down in South America.

A token of affection for the wonderful man who had always treated him kind while his late wife had spoiled him rotten with her home-baked sweets when he'd been a child.

It had been years since he'd seen the old Witch, and Javi was looking forward to it. His brother had recently inherited all of the property that had been held in their parents' trust for him down in Quito, Ecuador, where they had both been born.

Gabriel was the rightful heir and, as the second son, Javier was free to leave and live his life as he saw fit. The possibilities were endless, but ultimately, he'd decided on moving to the states. North America had always been his favorite vacation ground, and now it was time to make it his home.

The word *home* was somewhat ominous for a young bachelor, but there it was—pushed into his head by his inner Bear who was feeling his years somewhat. The great beast had been thinking about settling, pushing ideas of cubs and family into Javi's mind. But that was nonsense. Javi was still too young.

Mate, the Bear shoved the word at him, but Javi shushed the great beast.

He'd been ignoring the silly animal's increasingly annoying thoughts for the past hour. For some reason, his Bear had mating on his mind, but it probably had more to do with the fact his uncle was a world renowned matchmaker.

Whatever.

There was plenty of time for that. Javi was going to concentrate on enjoying himself for now. It was the Christmas season after all, and although Uncle Uzzi had tried to get him to use his famous Magical Matchmaking Service for years, Javier did not need to get mated right away.

His brother, Gabriel, on the other hand, could use his help. In fact, it was part of the reason he was there, to invite Uncle Uzzi down to the large Auberon family villa.

Javier was staying at a local hotel for the time being, but he intended on asking Uncle Uzzi for help finding an ideal town for his relocation. It was fast, but that was the way of things, There was just no place for him in the villa now that his brother had inherited the land and titles.

Javi bore him no ill will, it was simply tradition for his species. Andean Bears did not live in Clans, but rather, they had small family groups where only one male—an Alpha and the heir to the title—stood to inherit.

Kind of like the aristocracy of old England, he thought ruefully.

His brother did not necessarily want to be addressed by his formal title, Baron Gabriel Auberon, but Javi did love to taunt the old boy.

"Javier Auberon," a familiar voice rang out. "Don't dawdle in the shadows. Come and say hello."

"Uncle Uzzi," he said, jogging up the steps to greet the man himself.

"Aha! There you are. It is so good to see you, *osito*," Uncle Uzzi appeared on the landing at the top of the large stone staircase that led to his enormous estate.

The old Witch looked elegant in his white and black tuxedo and sparkling blue eyes. The powers he used so well seemed to circle him in a million dazzling lights, but they dwindled as he shook his head nonchalantly and grabbed Javi's shoulders, giving them a friendly squeeze.

"The place looks spectacular, Uncle Uzzi. But it always does when you are hosting," Javi remarked, and took in the spectacular holiday decorations.

There were millions of twinkle lights, all in silvers and golds, with matching bows, and gorgeous evergreen boughs gracing the entryway.

"Thank you, *osito*. I do love the holidays, even if my liebling is not with me," he replied and Javi nodded, patting his arm affectionately.

"For you, Uncle," he said, presenting the older Witch with the special vintage wine he'd brought from his home country.

Uncle Uzzi accepted the box and peeked at the label.

"You found another bottle of my Betty's favorite. This is very special to me, Javier. Thank you."

"I am glad you like it."

"Of course, I do. Now, tell me, how is Gabriel? Things settling in at the villa?"

"He is very well, but it is such a big place for one lonely Bear. To be honest, he is having a difficult time finding his mate," Javier told Uncle Uzzi. "In fact, the new Baron has asked me to extend you an invitation to his villa for the new year, perhaps?"

"I see. Yes, I would love to visit Gabriel." Uzzi nodded, though his gaze seemed to stray for a split-second before he gave a final nod of assent. "Now, tell me more about you, dear boy. Where are you staying?"

Javier grinned as he made the rounds with Uncle Uzzi, bringing the older Witch up to speed on his life and decisions. He told him all about his search for a place of his own.

"Having chosen to move to the States, I am now looking for the perfect town to relocate. I have no use for busy cities or crowded spaces, you know my Bear will not like that, besides I can run my business virtually from anywhere I choose."

"I see. Any ideas?" Uzzi asked.

Javi shrugged, accepting a glass of eggnog from a passing server. The band was playing, people were milling about, and every room in the old place was decorated, featuring a different holiday theme. Uzzi preferred to honor all traditions, and every creed, culture, and supernatural legend was represented in the most tactful and tasteful ways.

"I just want to enjoy life," Javier told him honestly. "My business is very good and pretty self-sufficient. I want a quiet little place where I can walk down the street and not have to fight a mob of people."

"I understand. Got a little famous, did you?" Uzzi laughed.

"Indeed. That's what happens when you make a billion dollars in your first year going live. You know, Uncle Uzzi, I spent a week in New York, and I swear I was almost trampled every time I left town, but I loved the pizza," he grinned.

"Well, *osito*, I think I have the perfect place for you, but we can discuss that after the ball. Go on inside and enjoy yourself, make sure you mingle."

"Thank you, Uncle Uzzi. *Feliz Navidad*," Javi replied before making his way inside.

Christmas was Javier's favorite time of year, and

his Uncle Uzzi sure knew how to throw a party. It was not like one of the dull holiday events he'd spent at other wealthy people's homes. This was warm, exciting, and fun. It reminded him of better days in the past, when he'd been carefree and certain of his place in the world.

Javi frowned, disliking the sudden morose turn of his thoughts. Music drifted pleasantly above the crowd, and the live band was quite good. His inner Bear chuffed inside his mind's eye, the playful beast had always liked music. The holiday carols were fitting with the season, and these were done quite well.

He was polite as he weaved through the crowd, all dressed in their holiday finest. There were many people in the ballroom, mostly Shifters. Some were dancing, many were standing and chatting, and even more were sitting at elegantly set tables being served by the smiling waitstaff.

There were tons of food featuring dishes from all over the world. Tiny finger sandwiches, delicate cheese puffs, quiches, salads, tamales, empanadas, pastas, sushi, and bite-sized chunks of grilled meats on tiny little skewers were being passed out by servers in waistcoats. There were bars discreetly in the corners, and servers with trays of punch for the children, and champagne or eggnog for the adults, walking through the rooms.

Javier was not starving. He was too amped up from his travels and wandered around instead. Much to his delight, it had been snowing when he'd arrived, and looking out one of the large windows, he was taken aback by the spectacular view.

The forest was blanketed in white, looking for all the world like the perfect Christmas card setting. Javier stopped as the sounds of tiny voices reached his ears and noted a separate room where a group of children were running happily amok.

It was just like Uncle Uzzi to include his guests' young. They had their own food and waitstaff present, but with so many little voices, he imagined it was difficult for the staff to hear everyone. He went inside to see if he could help.

The cubs and pups seemed thrilled to be there, and why not? They had their very own entertainment area with a DJ, cookie decorating tables and, of course, some lucky volunteer dressed as Santa himself. Javier went inside, unable to help himself.

Just for a few moments.

He always enjoyed being around the children of the staff at his brother's villa. He had once even considered going to school to become a teacher. His father had even encouraged him, but Javier soon found his love for business rivaled that of teaching other people's children.

No, he would save all his affection for when he was a father himself. Something he hadn't thought about very much till right then, but he sure could picture it. A small cub to play catch with or a sweet girl to cherish and spoil. Either way, he would love his cubs more than anything—he just knew it.

"That's mine!"

"No, it's mine!"

"Easy, *ninos*, tell me, what is the problem?" Javier asked and kneeled down to speak with the two small children, who were arguing over what appeared to be a bowl of silver sprinkles.

"I was usin' them first!" One adorable cherub pouted angrily.

"Nuh uh!" returned the other freckled sprite.

"I see. Well, did you both know that everything is much more fun when we share? Look, here is another bowl with even more wonderful colors," he told them. Javi smiled when the kids appeared stunned, and he placed another small dish of the delightful confections between the two children. Next, he handed them spoons.

Within seconds, they were both enthusing over

their cookies, and they even promised to make one for Javier himself. He laughed indulgently and stood back up.

"*Gracias*. I look forward to enjoying them," he said and waved as he walked back out to the main hallway.

Children were a blessing, and he did want them someday. The only problem was, he needed a female to get them.

Mate, cried his Bear.

Chapter Five

"Uncle Uzzi really outdid himself," a slender woman said as she walked by and pointed at the décor.

Javi had to agree. The mansion looked like a winter wonderland in his humble opinion. There were twinkle lights everywhere and thick pine garland with velvet bows and sparkles. Nope. There was no mistaking his uncle's love for the season. It showed in every corner of the place, from the large snowmen and reindeer displays, to the small snowflake-shaped ice cubes that floated in the drinks.

The Christmas decorations were a mix of traditional and new age, and he had to hand it to his Uncle Uzzi, he was simply a master at this. Hosting parties, decorations, food, music were some of his many talents.

He recalled the times when he'd come to visit them down in Quito. His wife, Aunt Betty, had been alive then, and she had helped his mother arrange parties and events for their neighbors with Uzzi right at her side, doing her bidding, he had learned from the best, and the tradition carried on. Javi could not be more pleased.

The sheer number of smiling guests was a testament to that, as it was to Uzzi's incredible matchmaking abilities if the whispers Javi was hearing were true. And, of course, they were. Shifters did not bother with lies.

Certainly impressive. He wondered if *all* the couples had his uncle to thank for their seemingly happy arrangements. More than likely, he decided.

There must have been three-hundred people, Shifters and normals alike, in the large ballroom. He smiled and introduced himself to a few of them who seemed nice enough.

Truth be told, Javier did not really like large crowds. Like most Andean Bear Shifters, he was a solitary sort of man. He admired the couples who seemed to ignore everyone else as they held hands and twirled along the dance floor.

So many happy pairs. He didn't like feeling envious of anyone, in fact, he often made it a point not to, but for a little while, Javi simply could not help it. Maybe he would take Uncle Uzzi up on his offer after all. Maybe it was time to settle down.

Mate, chuffed his Bear.

Yes, he wanted a mate of his own. Someone to love and cherish, to build a life with. It was a nice dream.

Mate, the Bear pushed the thought at him, a little bit harder this time.

At first, Javi had thought it was his silly beast pushing his own agenda into Javier's brain. But then, with no warning at all, Javier's skin began to burn. He felt hot all over, and his Bear was growling incessantly inside of him. His heart was beating heavily inside his chest—like a jackhammer trying to break through his tailored suit.

Inside his mind's eye, he saw his Bear stand on his hind legs. The familiar spectacled face of his animal was quite serious as a growl built up inside of his chest and exploded through his lips.

Those nearest him turned, and Javi quickly cut off the sound. Then it hit him—the most delicious fragrance he had ever smelled. His head whipped around to find the location of that crazy good scent

—cinnamon sugar with hints of citrus. It was so familiar to him, and yet, he knew he'd never come across it before.

Wait a second—it was like freshly made *bunuelos* —his favorite holiday dessert. Javier's mouth watered even as he recognized the scent was not coming from any of the trays the waitstaff was passing around to the crowd. Following his nose, Javier raced through the crowds.

Sniff, sniff, sniff. Stop. There.

He paused and had to bite back his roar when he found the source of the tantalizing fragrance. His skin tingled, stomach clenched, and Bear roared inside of him.

Mine.

The stunning female was the source of the delectable fragrance, but she was surrounded by two males, one on either side of her luscious figure. The fact she appeared disinterested—*bored even*—as they tried and failed to engage her attention was the only thing that saved those two men from being mauled by his beast.

Taking a moment to regain control over his Bear, Javier raked the luscious beauty from head to toe with his gaze. She stood about five-foot nine-inches tall, which put her half a foot shorter than himself.

Perfect for reaching down to nuzzle her sinfully sexy little mouth, he thought, and smiled as he took her in. She was beyond words, so pretty, so fine. He liked the way her top lip was slightly fuller than the lower —a lure just to tempt him.

Sexy sweet female. So luscious, so lovely.

Javi seemed frozen in time and space. His mind churned with a million different things he wanted to say and do to his beautiful heart's desire. He could not wait to spend hours learning what pleased her. He hoped she enjoyed long, hot, wet kisses. With a mouth like that, he could just imagine nibbling on it for days on end.

Her body was curvy and splendid, gloriously outlined by the gown she wore. The neckline was a plunging v that left her high, full breasts covered by two scraps of iridescent material. The rest of the dress had an empire waist with a long skirt that fell to her ankles in layers of more of that same mesmer-izing fabric.

Holy fuck.

His pants grew tight around the sudden hardness hidden behind the expertly tailored pants. Thank goodness, or he'd have punched right through them by now. He gave his cock a discreet thump to calm the fucking thing down. With any luck, it went unnoticed by the other guests.

Fuck, she was something. He was desperate to get closer to the beauty. Yes, she was beautiful. Simply stunning really, but it was more than the gorgeous gown that appeared as if she'd been encased in a piece of the night sky—as if the gods themselves had known she was much too special for any earthly material. And it was more than her glossy brown curls and the long, sexy slip of her neck. There was something else about her. An aura of light lit from deep inside that spoke of her innate goodness and called to the Bear within him.

She was enough to stop a man's heart dead inside his chest, and he wanted her. With each passing second, his desire grew, and Javi had to grit his teeth against the possessive growl that rumbled in his throat.

She smiled politely at the two males vying for her attentions, but Javi knew bored when he saw it. The woman was not at all entertained.

Poor darling, he thought, gazing at the sexy and lithe vixen. Her voluptuousness was drool worthy and had caught many of the attending Shifters' eyes, to Javi's immediate consternation. But, like the two idiots surrounding her, she had ignored them all.

The would be suitors attempted to tell a joke, but his sweet mate's smile went cold. It did not quite reach her eyes, and Javi's Bear scratched at his skin once more as he took in the situation.

Why should she continue to be bored by them? A very good question, and his Bear was half a second from kicking his own ass to get him moving. His sweet *querida* was not having a good time at all and Javi should remedy that. The poor sods didn't know it, but this beautiful woman was not there for them. She was there for him.

Mine, confirmed his inner beast in a deep resounding growl that resonated in his soul.

"Thank you, Uncle Uzzi," Javier whispered, and his mind flashed an image of the cunning old Witch.

He grinned at his Uncle's meddling. It seemed that even without leave, the brilliant matchmaker had done it again.

Lucky Javi.

"So, I was wondering if maybe you would like to dance?"

Javier listened to the unknown Shifter ask his mate to dance and began to move towards her, but it seemed the gorgeous little, *sniff,* she-Tiger did not need his intervention.

"No, thank you. I apologize, but I need to run, if

you would please excuse me," she returned and smiled tightly.

The she-Cat walked away from the two males, who had smelled distinctly like some kind of lizard to Javier's Bear.

"Damn, Zircon, that woman was fine," said one of the men.

"Easy Dor. Look, bro, relax. We didn't even get her name," he said, and Javi realized he was talking to him.

Hands raised, they faced him and waited. Javier shook his head and stopped growling at the guys.

"Sorry, my dude," the other one said. "We didn't know she was spoken for. Happy Holidays, man."

"Excuse me, gentlemen." Javier nodded at them and turned to find the woman.

He appreciated the fact that she had—in no uncertain terms—turned down the strangers. His Bear would've liked to make sure they understood she was off limits, but he was not there to make trouble for any of Uncle Uzzi's guests.

Still, it was probably for the best she had not wanted to dance with them. At least now, Javier wouldn't have to ruin his suit by beating some strange man's brains in for touching his unclaimed mate.

Grrr. Possessive? Yep.

He needed to find her. Javi just had to introduce himself, but unfortunately, she was walking in the opposite direction. He had to hustle just to catch up. This really was going to be the best Christmas ever. New home, new mate, new life. Javi hummed a tune as he chased his mate down the hall.

Not a creature was stirring, except for a Bear chasing his mate...

Chapter Six

Pamela took a turn in a quieter section of the mansion after being regaled by two of the most uninteresting dolts she had ever run across. Why would she care about how some Shifter sports league was doing?

Whatever.

She was, however, amazed at how beautiful Uncle Uzzi's mansion was and not just because it was filled with gorgeous Shifters, and glittery, magical decorations. The structure itself was simply breathtaking. Especially to a woman who'd never really had much of a home. It was simply spectacular.

Pamela would not lie, she had been nervous when she arrived. After the initial shock that she,

Pamela Brown, had been chosen to represent their Pride at this special gathering of Uncle Uzzi's most beloved clients had worn off, she unwound a bit.

When was the last time Pam had been able to really celebrate anything? Paulie was her whole life, and keeping him safe, healthy, and happy was her pride and privilege. Being a mother was the most special thing she could be, but Pamela was also a woman.

Blake had stolen that from her, and tonight, she was determined to begin the journey to get it back. Slowly, oh so slowly, she was coming back into herself—the self that had been denied by a controlling bastard.

No more. He gets no more of me.

The second she thought the words, Pamela felt as if a weight had been lifted. A grin spread across her face, and she felt all abuzz, like the promise of joy was tingling against her skin. Head back, she took in the amazing decoration Uzzi had provided.

The mansion was a winter wonderland with countless twinkle lights indoors and outside, sparkling like a million fairies were dancing in the air. She giggled like a schoolgirl, spinning round in a circle as she finally made the decision to let go of the tethers to her past hurts.

It was Christmas, after all, and the trees were decorated, the eggnog was flowing, and the sounds of carols filled every room of this place.

Time to start having fun, Pamela, she told herself. *Time to start living.*

All the razzle dazzle holiday glitz was stunning, but Pamela's favorite part of the evening was walking through the empty rooms. She was not exactly avoiding the partygoers—which would have been odd, since at one time people would have thought she was the ultimate party girl.

It was more that she liked the quiet and the space. Her Tiger could breathe better when she was alone. Pamela had learned to love herself over the past year, and it was a beautiful thing. She did not hate crowds or parties, but she did not crave attention either. Sometimes, Pam wondered what she would have been had she never fallen in with the wrong crowd.

Party girl? Nah. Geeky girl? Maybe. Snort.

She'd taken to borrowing books from the girls of the Pride and had found a few favorites among indie authors who self-published. Amazing, really, how these writers made a business of thoughts and words. She found it fascinating, not to mention entertaining as hell. Who would have guessed she was a closet romance reader?

Crazier things had happened, she supposed. Pam ran her fingertips along a silvery curtain that was hanging from a crystal rod above a floor to ceiling window. She gazed outside at the gorgeously land-scaped gardens behind Uncle Uzzi's mansion.

He had his people decorate put there too. Two lovers kissed in a dark corner, and Pamela bit her lower lip, turning away before things got heated. She sighed and kept on strolling. The couple deserved privacy, even if a tiny part of her was feeling a little bit jealous. Must be nice to find someone to love. That had never been her destiny, though.

"Onward," she whispered to herself, taking time to appreciate the quieter spaces.

She was still thinking about all the wasted time putting on airs and pretense for others, and she didn't want to. The past was the past, and Pamela had only the future in front of her now. That was the kind of positive thinking that she worked on with others in the Maverick Point Support Group. A mantra of sorts, but it helped many get through days when everything seemed too dark and cold to handle.

Pamela was in a good place now, emotionally,

mentally, and physically. She did more than alright for herself and Paulie. The small apartment they rented was just fine for the two of them, but looking around at all this splendor, she had to wonder if she was doing it wrong. What she wouldn't give to have so much space.

Chuff.

Her Tiger was right, this was too much, but Pamela would love a home where Paulie could play in the backyard. One that was big enough for a tree fort and swing set. Maybe a pool for summertime. Contrary to popular opinion, some cats—*Tigers especially*—loved to swim.

The apartment building where they lived only had a small concrete courtyard, but they were within walking distance of the community park, so that was good. She'd converted her former bedroom into a room for her son. He needed a bigger space for his desk and toys. Now that he was in school, they had redecorated, painting it together in bright primary colors. Of course, Paulie had gotten more paint on himself than on the actual walls.

Silly cub.

Her heart squeezed whenever she thought of her sweet boy. He looked like Pamela, with soft brown curls and big bright eyes. She didn't think she ever looked so young, but she must have.

Sleeping on the pullout couch was worth it to see his grin when she'd told him he was getting his own big boy room. Pam didn't mind at all. Her cub was growing up fast and needed it more than she did.

Thank goodness she'd made amends with her Neta and Nari. The Pride would always be there for him should anything happen to her, and the thought comforted Pamela.

The band was striking up again, this time playing *Santa Baby* and Pamela hummed along with the saucy tune. She wandered into a room that was done in silvers and blues and was struck by the beauty.

She thought Christmas was supposed to be all greens and reds, but Uncle Uzzi seemed to favor the winter wonderland look, and she was happy for it. A tall, perfect Christmas tree sat in the corner—one of the dozens of live Christmas trees Uncle Uzzi had decorated throughout the house. This one was her favorite, she decided right then. It was decorated with ornaments shaped like crystal icicles, with thousands of glowing white and blue lights glowing behind them like something out of a fairy tale. A thick, blue velvet skirt surrounded the bottom half, and she grinned, having learned each tree was complete with its root ball so it could be planted later.

The tree at the Pride House was the same, only it held a mishmash of homemade ornaments and multi-colored lights. It was homey, but beautiful—only in a very different way from this one.

Pamela appreciated both. She circled the enormous thing, touching the needles with her fingertips, careful not to dislodge any of the crystal ornaments. It was beautiful, but even so, she preferred the small one back in her apartment. The one that proudly displayed all the little ornaments Paulie had made her over the years.

Yeah, that was definitely her favorite.

Pamela checked her cell phone and saw the latest pic Hunter and Elissa had sent her of Paulie and his friends eating popcorn and watching a classic animated Christmas movie. She smiled warmly at the image and dropped the phone back into one of the cleverly hidden pockets of her gown.

She'd have to tell Jessica when she got back that no less than six women had asked her where she'd purchased the beautiful ensemble. The ladies of her Pride were so talented—amazing, really, and she was glad to know them.

Jessica's Closet was a tremendous success. As was

the lingerie line, *Kisses By Kylie*, that was Doc Mikey's mate's business. *Cut It Out*, Gretchen's salon, and the place of Pamela's employment, was seeing clients from within a 75-mile radius now. That was a long way to drive for highlights, but people loved them. Yeah, those women were special, and Pamela was forever indebted to them.

With their help, she'd gotten a good job and her cub was happier than ever. She only hoped this Christmas would erase the past few where she'd had almost nothing to give her precious son. She bit her lip and thought about the following day when she would pick up her last paycheck before the holidays. She planned to go shopping right after.

Elissa had volunteered to watch Paulie so she could cross off a few of the things on his Christmas list. The toy truck and building blocks were easy enough, but there were some things neither Pamela nor Santa could buy. His carefully printed Christmas list flashed in her mind. One word on that list caused her heart to constrict, and she almost sobbed aloud, thinking about it.

. . .

D*ear Santa,*

I really want a new building block set so I can build Mommy a big house. Maybe I can get a toy truck to carry the bricks. Also, I was really good this year, so maybe you can also bring me a dad. All my friends have one, and I need someone to play catch with and maybe a little brother, too. I promise to be good.

Love,

Paulie B.

Holy forking fart balls, reading that had almost broken her. Paulie wanted a family for Christmas. It was one thing she couldn't give him, and it broke her heart. She shook her head and wiped the tear that had trickled down her cheek. That was a problem for another day. Pamela was not there to wallow, she was there to have a nice time.

Determined, she pushed all her sadness right out of her head. Tonight, she was having fun. She thought back on the elaborate sit down dinner Uncle Uzzi had provided for his guests. The food was wonderful, and though it pained her, Pamela made small talk to those around her. She'd eaten and smiled, albeit a little stiffly, at the few unattached males who'd sat near her.

She was grateful when the meal ended, and she

was free to walk around again. Her smiles had been misconstrued by two rather stubborn males who'd dogged her every step, but she was still trying to have a good time.

Finally, she was able to get away from them, but not before she noticed another male who'd seemed a little too interested. Of course, that one was different. Ridiculously handsome with bronzed skin and stylishly messy black locks that hung rakishly over his forehead. The first thing she'd noted about his appearance were those crazy gorgeous locks—*and images of her long nails combing through that hair immediately flashed inside her head.*

Eeek...down girl!

The stranger watched her with dark eyes that glittered like black diamonds in the dimly lit hall. He seemed overly interested in her conversation with the other two males, but there was something about his predator's gaze that set him apart from the rest. Pamela had easily dismissed the two men, failing to engage her in conversation, but this one. He was different.

Grrr.

Something about him had her she-Tiger panting with need. She'd never felt quite like that before. Horny—sure—but desperate to have his cock stretching her and filling her five seconds after they locked eyes with one another? No. That was not the norm for Pamela.

His gaze raked her over from head to toe, and she sucked in a breath. She felt exposed—naked, even though her gown was still intact.

Dangerous.

Yes, he was that. Dangerous, sexy, and damn, was he good-looking. Powerfully built, larger than any of the males in the Pride, he was all bronzed muscles and smoldering eyes. The scent of pine trees and mountain air reached her sensitive nostrils and her Tiger growled louder, causing Pamela to tremble in her skin. Heat pooled between her legs and her she-Cat pushed to come out. Her inner animal hissed a single word and Pamela froze.

Mine.

Chapter Seven

Uh oh.

This was not happening. So not fucking happening.

Maybe the fucking can happen?

She scolded her she-Tiger—the feline was horny as an old goat, for fuck's sake. But this was not the night of meaningless sex Elissa had told her to enjoy. This was something else.

Panic filled her chest as she listened to the man approach and heard him inhale deeply. A sexy little growl played in his throat, making her crazy with lust. Her pulse raced as he inched closer, and the woodsy scent clinging to his custom tux made her want to rub herself all over it.

Mate.

Gulp.

Keep it down, kitty. He is not for us.

Yes, he is. Mate, her she-Tiger growled insistently.

"Holy forking fart balls of fire," she huffed one of Paulie's favorite non-curses.

"Pardon?" the male asked, eyebrow raised and a stupidly handsome grin quirking one corner of his mouth up.

She wanted to reach up and lick him right there. Shit. She was so screwed.

"Nothing," she muttered, trying to compose herself.

Most Shifters dreamt of the day they'd meet their fated mates, but Pamela had been down this road before. She'd given everything she had to a man and had been used and abused.

Fucking Blake, she shivered in disgust at the thought of the madman's name. The things she'd done and had been subjected to under the influence of the former Beta of the Maverick Pride—*the man who had duped them all but her most of all*—used to make Pamela want to weep with shame.

But. Not. Anymore.

Not since she'd learned she had real friends in the Pride. They'd showed her kindness and patience and she knew now that she had nothing to be ashamed of. Pamela had been a victim of Blake's dishonesty and cruelty.

She thought she loved him, and he took advantage of her affection. He'd tricked her into thinking he was her mate and had used her and others horribly, but she would not regret it. That would mean regretting Paulie, and she would never, ever do that.

Her son was the most important thing in her life. She had steady work now at *Cut It Out*, friends, and a chance to make a place for herself and her son in the Pride. Being asked to come here to this event to represent them was an honor and, like Elissa said, she was going to make the most of it.

When was the last time she'd gotten dressed up and let her hair down? Never like this, she thought nervously and looked down at the beautiful dress Jessica had loaned her.

But this man threatened all of that. Here was danger. A mate could be demanding. He would want to turn her life upside down. There were too many possibilities.

The stranger stood still some inches away from her, but she felt heat coming off of him like he was a bloody furnace. Her panties were positively soaked at this point and the pleasant rumble coming from him grew louder.

The fucker knew what he was doing.

She'd worked so hard to make her life better, but she never thought she would have a fated mate. Maybe it didn't mean what she thought it meant. Maybe it could last for the evening alone.

Pamela worried her lower lip between her teeth. She had no intention of being tied to a man ever again. The large male leaned closer and sniffed the sensitive skin along her neck, his growl grew louder.

"Beautiful, *querida*," he murmured, and her sex throbbed in need.

Fart balls.

She should be angry, but she didn't think he did it on purpose. If what she had scented was real, the stranger was just as helpless as she was. Either way, she needed to confront it—to confront him.

Her mate.

Pamela straightened her shoulders and turned abruptly, running right smack into his pretty formidable chest. When the heck had he moved?

Strong arms wrapped around her waist to steady her, and she gripped the lapels of the exquisite suit jacket tightly as the scent of sunshine, pine trees, and fresh mountain air reached her nostrils.

Dear gods!

She swayed as the delicious scent seemed to send

shockwaves of awareness careening through her blood. Her Tiger panted, moisture pooled at her center, and her blood roared in her ears.

Oh no. Not this.

Sometimes feline Shifters experience an influx of their heat cycle when confronted with their mates. Not always. But sometimes. Need burned between her legs, and if she didn't see to it soon, the pain would start.

Sniff, the big male leaned closer, pulling her into the cradle of his enormous, hard body. Fuck, that felt better. She was still turned on, but his touch soothed the Cat.

"Easy, *querida,* I've got you," his slightly accented voice whispered into her ear.

Pamela trembled involuntarily as she tried to clench her thighs, hoping the pressure would ease some of her need. That sexy, growly voice was filling her head with all sorts of naughty ideas. She moaned softly and licked her lips, unable to stop her temperature from spiking. His eyes flashed, and she knew what conclusion he'd drawn from that slow intake of air, because the truth was, Pamela had come to the same one.

Mate. Mine. Need. Uh oh.

"My name is Javier Auberon, and you, sweet kitten, are *mine*."

Pamela's eyes traveled up past his massive chest and shoulders to the perfectly trimmed shadow on his face, all the way until she reached his cocky grin and glittering eyes. The easy confidence in his stare shook her, and she narrowed her own at him.

"I'm sorry," she said. "I think you've mistaken me for a toy or a possession. I don't belong to you. I don't belong to anyone," she replied, pulling out of his arms and, of course, she immediately missed his warmth.

"No, I am not wrong. You belong to me, *kitten*. I can smell your need. Why deny it?" he asked, and she felt his confusion.

"Nuh uh," she shook her head. "I have worked too hard for my life."

"And I long to hear about it, but your heat. It is starting, yes? Let me help," he murmured, concern narrowing his gaze as a cramp hit her hard.

Damn.

The man was weaving spells around her with hardly any effort. Pamela was not a foolish kid any longer. She was not going to be caught up in this rush of hormones—no matter what the Fates decided. This she-Cat was not going to fall for him or any man ever again.

"Please, your pain is like my own. I apologize if I said something wrong. Will you at least allow me to walk with you? See if it passes?" He followed her down the hall, and she was powerless to stop him.

Fart balls.

Every second in his presence was temptation itself, and she knew it was only a matter of time before her heat really kicked in. That little biological nuisance happened with feline Shifters more frequently than with others to ensure propagation of the species. Fuck, it was already too late. Her stomach tightened and her sex clenched, She moaned softly.

Pamela couldn't trust herself not to jump him as it was. Sure, Elissa and Jess had joked about her getting her freak on tonight, but sex was something she'd gone a long time without. It was kind of hard to trust someone after what she'd been through.

But tell that to her needy little clit. The bud throbbed inside her silk panties and her channel clenched again on air desperate to be filled as Javier's mountain fresh musk filled her nostrils once more.

Double forking fart balls.

"Why do you want to do this?" she asked.

"You know why, kitten. Need you," he whispered, lips grazing her ear.

"Fine. One night, but that is all I'm promising," she said recklessly, and led him down the hall and away from the crowds.

"One night is all I need," he growled.

A small, secret part of Pamela hoped he didn't mean it. But that was something she would never admit.

"One night," she repeated, and closed her eyes against another, stronger wave of need.

Gulp.

Chapter Eight

"Where are you taking me?" he asked her, not really concerned, only that it was taking long, and he was desperate to touch her.

Javier watched her hips sway seductively in the dream of a gown she wore. His mate—thank the gods, he had finally met his mate, and she was gorgeous. He couldn't wait to undress her. Visions of fucking her on top of the shimmery gown had filled his head ever since he'd laid eyes on her. His own sweet kitten.

"I don't know, but I hope we get there soon," the woman of his every fantasy laughed, and it was like silver bells sounding through the air.

For a moment, he thought he could hear her

underlying sorrow, and that bothered his Bear. He wanted her happy. No, he wanted her overjoyed, as he was to finally meet her. *His mate.* The one person in the universe designed wholly and completely for him.

She tried the doorknob of the first room at the top of a deserted stairwell and met his eyes when it clicked. Javier exhaled slowly, relieved that the room was unlocked.

"This must be a guestroom," the gorgeous she-Tiger said as they walked inside the neat little bedroom.

It was clean, but unoccupied. They both would've scented any person who might have slept there recently, but everything was fresh and new. That was good. His Bear did not like the idea of her on anyone else's sheets or furniture.

She was too precious for that. His throat rumbled with his animal as Javier ran his fingers down her bare arms once she'd stopped walking. He'd never thought himself particularly lucky, but Javi must have been blessed to deserve such a treasure as she. His mate stood in front of the tall window, bathed in moonlight like a goddess. Her beauty unparalleled.

"Your skin is lovely. So soft and pale," he murmured and ducked his head to taste it.

He'd been dying to see if she was as sweet as he imagined, and she was. Sweeter still. No longer able to hold back, he spun her in his arms and breathed in her cinnamon sugar scent in great big gulps. Like a greedy child who couldn't wait to gobble up all his treats—but Javier knew better than to rush this. She was his mate, and he would savor her like the treasure she was.

"Feels good," she whimpered, and he smiled widely. He wanted to please her. It was imperative.

"I'm dying to taste you," he growled, placing biting kisses along her jaw till he reached her mouth.

Javier trembled like a green boy as he reached for her, cupping her cheeks in his hands. She was so beautiful. He bent his head to capture her mouth, unable to delay, not even for a moment. Fuck, her top lip was as delectable as he'd imagined earlier.

She moaned and opened for him, and his cock hardened even more. Her instinctive submission to his seeking tongue was making him so damn hot. Their kiss turned frantic as his feisty little mate reached for his jacket and tugged it off, next came his shirt. Ignoring the last few buttons, Javier pulled the thing off, burning to have her hands on his skin.

She wanted him, and the knowledge made him drunk. He growled and nipped at her skin, loving the way she purred in response. Desire was good between mates, necessary even. She'd said one night, and he agreed only because he had a plan. Javier was going to make her addicted to him.

He was going to love on her so damn good she would not want the night to end. And when dawn finally came, she would be his for all time.

It was a good plan. A fucking great one, as far as he was concerned. Running on instinct, he cupped her breasts, squeezing the ripe mounds, testing their weight. She was all woman, and his Bear was already enamored. Sexy, elegant, and earthy at the same time.

Perfect. Sexy. Mine.

"Fuck, kitten, you taste so damn good," he growled and swallowed her lusty moan.

The scent of her arousal increased, teasing his senses, making his cock throb inside his pants, and filling him with all manner of naughty little images. Javier was going to see each one become reality, but first, he was going to make his sweet mate purr.

She pushed at his shoulders and Javi's eyes snapped to hers, breaking the kiss. He noted her swollen lips with satisfaction. His gorgeous mate reached behind her and undid the clasp of her gown, tugging the two straps down and unveiling the best damn present he ever got for Christmas.

Holy fucking hell. She was stunning. Javier's growl reverberated in the room as she released her breasts from their confines.

"Mine," he whispered in a deep, guttural voice that was more Bear than man. He could not help it.

"For tonight," she agreed, and he said nothing.

Her bosoms were rounded and full, with dark tips that hardened under his fervent stare. He moved in, desperate to get his hands on them, but knowing she needed tenderness and reverence. Javier cupped her, teasing the tight buds with his fingers while he mashed his lips to hers once more.

His naughty little kitten rubbed her tongue against his in a way that had his balls tightening, seeking release as he pressed his hard length against her soft belly. Christ, she was so damn hot. Made him positively wild with her pants and moans. He needed more. Needed her. Could not wait to sink into her.

"Yes," she growled softly as his lips sought her earlobe, then her neck, and finally closed over one ripe tip.

The growly little purring sound was almost his undoing. Javi teased the nubbin with his tongue, tugging it gently with his teeth and releasing one to suckle the other. Her fingers pulled on his hair, and fuck if that wasn't pushing him closer to the edge.

Naughty little kitten, like a little hair pulling, eh?

Good thing Javi did too. Nothing was taboo as long as those involved were willing, and for his mate, he would do anything and everything to see to her pleasure.

"Need you naked," he grunted.

Javi closed his eyes, battling the Bear. His animal was pushing for control. He wanted to mark her, to claim his mate right then and there, but first, he needed her consent, and she was already under the mistaken impression that this was a one-night thing. That was his fault.

Liar liar.

No. Not a lie. I will make her want me so much, she will not let go. She is mine. Mate.

Javier hadn't lied. Okay, maybe a little, but only because she did not understand his meaning. He'd said he only needed one night, but he meant to make her change her mind. It was the only reason he had gotten away with it. Otherwise, her Tiger would have known.

Most Shifters didn't lie because they could detect it in a person's scent and see it in their body language. Subtle changes, like the nuance in a person's voice could give away a lie easily.

So no, he had not lied when he said he only needed one night. He just did not mean what she thought he meant. Now that he had her in his arms, Javier knew he would never let her go.

This female was his, decreed by the Fates, and he was hers as well. She was his whole universe—everything to him. Javier had means and determination on his side. He would win her love if it took forever.

Starting now, he growled, his body on fire for the sexy she-Tiger. She was the only one capable of cooling the flame of his need. And fuck, yes, he needed her, wanted her, had to have her.

Mine. Mine. MINE.

Okay, so his Bear was a possessive asshole. Who could blame him? There would be no one else for Javi. Only her.

"Like this, sweet?"

"Yes, oh yes," she moaned, her head back as he licked a trail down her breasts to her belly, nipping the scrap of cloth that covered her most secret place before trailing kisses along her delicious thighs.

He wanted every one of her shivers and trembles, every purr and moan from her luscious mouth. Possessive, she'd mentioned that, and maybe he was about her, but he knew she was no toy or bauble. She was a fucking goddess and if she let him, he would worship at her feet.

"Javier?"

"Yes."

"Would you do something for me?"

"Anything," he returned, stopping the kiss he'd been planting along her inner left leg. Her scent was strong, he knew she wanted him, would have known it even if he wasn't able to see that little bit of fabric damp with her need from his position on his knees and almost all the way between her thighs.

"Will you stop if I say so?" she asked, and he knew it was important to her.

"Of course," he nodded, answering honestly.

It might kill him, but Javier would most certainly stop if that was what she wanted. His mate's needs and desires came first. Always.

"Do you want me to stop, *querida?*" he asked, and fuck, he was panting.

"No. I was just checking." The sexy little temptress grinned and bit her lip.

"Good," he growled, standing, and lifting her off the floor in one move. He needed that mouth under his, had to kiss the teasing little delight that she was.

She moaned aloud and clung to his shoulders

while he found and placed her on a plush armchair. He stepped back to take her in, bare-breasted, and her dress pushed up around her waist.

"What are you doing?" she asked, but she didn't seem worried.

Javier nudged her legs gently and the sexy vixen opened them for him as he kneeled back down and pushed the silky fabric of her skirt even higher, revealing her silk-covered sex. The material was dark where her honey had saturated it, and fuck, he was dying for a taste.

Javi's hands trailed up her smooth legs, circling to her inner thighs and brushing the edges of those naughty little panties. Black silk with the tiniest hint of lace, so fine, they were almost sheer. Up and down, he drew tiny circles on her skin, marking the flesh there with his touch.

"Please," she begged, flexing her hips as another wave of heat hit her.

That was the thing about felines. When the females went into heat, any healthy male within a hundred yards felt the call. But she was all his, and Javier was not into sharing. He would take care of her, now, tomorrow, always. She whimpered involuntarily as his seeking fingers crept closer to their goal.

"Don't you know, querida, you can have anything you want," he growled, and used his shoulders to hold her legs open.

Keeping her gaze, Javi bent his head and closed his lips over her needy sex, suckling her through the damp fabric. His mate hissed aloud as her cinnamon sugar honey exploded on his tongue. There was no stopping him now. Javi was ravenous for her.

Popping a single claw from his pinky, he sliced through her panties, careful of her skin, and devoured her fragrant musk. Fuck, she was divine, and all he wanted to do was rub his face and tongue all over her slick folds. To stamp himself there, and pleasure her like only he could.

Her pussy was so pretty, so pink, with closely cropped dark curls. He reached out with the flat of his tongue, lapping at her warm honey. Then, because he could not stop his beast from joining, he used his Bear's ability to extend his lips, curling on around her clit. Fuck yes, she liked that if her little moans and the tightening of her fingers in his hair told him anything.

Javi growled, eating her with gusto. Then she did it, his mate began to purr, her body vibrating like crazy as he fucked her with his mouth. The deep, rumbly sound had him reaching between his own legs and opening his slacks. Javi stroked his cock once and squeezed it hard. Hoping to knock some sense into his dick before he came right there.

Fuck, she was potent. He added first one, then two fingers to stretch her tight channel, nibbling her tiny little nubbin for all he was worth until she bucked mindlessly against him. Javier growled as her sheath tightened on his fingers and her orgasm exploded on his tongue.

"So good," he growled, lapping at her dripping slit until he'd swallowed every last drop.

"Oh, gods." She sighed and leaned back, her golden gaze meeting his.

Fuck, he thought, *please say you want me too.*

He would do as she wished—anything she wished.

"Do you want me to stop?" he asked, unable to wait a moment longer.

"Stop? Oh no, I don't want you to stop, Javi. I want to feel your cock inside of me, filling me, now," she growled and moved so fast he hardly saw it happen.

One minute he was kneeling at the apex of her thighs, the next she'd shoved him down onto the floor and was straddling his hips and rubbing her slick pussy all over his cock. Javi could hardly breathe as she lifted up and took him inside her molten sheath. Her amber eyes glowed gold as her she-Tiger reached out to meet his Bear.

Mine.

"S'good," she moaned, taking him deep, deep, deeper still.

Javier grunted and sat up, thrusting upwards. He was beyond words now, instinct taking over, he bucked and reveled in the glory of her body while she rode him like the goddess she was. Her throaty moans and purring noises were music to his ears, and he looked forward to a lifetime of hearing them.

Fingers tipped with his claws, he squeezed her hips, piercing the flesh there, giving her the first of his mating marks. She might not have said yes entirely, but his Bear was stealing some of his control while his sweet mate fucked him stupid.

She moaned in response to his scratches, a fresh wave of moisture coated his cock as she encompassed him. Her muscles squeezed, adjusting to his size and girth.

"Take me deep, kitten. I want your pussy sucking my cock forever. That's it, ride me hard, harder, fuck yes, *querida*," he growled, switching from English to Spanish as he praised her efforts and peppered her with kisses and passionate declarations.

"Javi," she called his name, and his arms tightened their hold around her.

Her inner muscles gripped him tightly. She was divine. Out of this world. And he was going to come any minute.

"Like that, yes kitten, you feel so fucking good," he grunted and latched on to one of her nipples as she began to move harder and faster.

Mine. Mine. Mine!

His Bear roared possessively as euphoria built higher and higher. Javier's heart beat a deafening tattoo as he poured everything he had, all his love, emotions, and promises for the future, into every kiss and stroke.

MATE!

Together, they writhed on the floor. Two desperate people, wild for one another. His cock stroked that spot deep inside, rubbing her good and hard, becoming one as they fucked until he felt her seep all the way into his very soul.

"Gonna come again," she groaned, and her movements became jerky and erratic.

Javier took over then. He picked her up and slammed her down on his cock. Fucking her deeper, harder, and more completely with every move. Her eyes were locked onto his, and for the life of him, he couldn't look away. He lost his heart in that moment.

Call him crazy, but Javier loved her already. He would never stop loving her, wanting her, needing her—not ever. He wanted her for keeps. Vowed to keep her right there, with his dick buried so deep she would not know where she ended, and he began.

Keep fucking her until she can't move. Until she can't even think of leaving me.

"Oh, fuck," she screamed as her sex squeezed him and he was right there with her, filling her to the brim with his cum, marking her with his scent.

"Wanna claim you," he growled around a mouth full of his Bear's teeth.

"No," she said breathlessly and shook her head. "I said yes to just one night."

"It's not enough, kitten," he said and cupped her face in his hands as his cock hardened inside of her once more.

"Oh fuck, yes," she moaned as he laid her down and moved inside her again. He was insatiable, and she was a feast for the senses. His senses.

"Look at me while I take you," he demanded, easing in and out of her slowly, carefully, allowing her to feel every inch of him throbbing and pulsing within her.

"Be mine, sweet kitten. Say yes," he murmured, but still the stubborn woman shook her head.

"You want this. Admit it," he added, and continued rocking his hips against hers in torturously slow circles.

"No," she said, meeting his stare and raking her nails down his back to cup his ass. "Now stop messing around and fuck me."

"What's wrong, kitten? Can't take the pressure?" Javi growled and pressed deeper, but just as slowly.

Withdraw, plunge, swivel, withdraw, plunge, swivel.

He fucked her slowly with long, deep strokes that sent lightning volts of sensation right to his cock. She fit him so perfectly, he never wanted to stop. He found her g-spot and stroked it long and hard until his little kitten was clawing at him, begging him for more.

"Please, faster, harder," she growled.

"What do you need, mate?" Javi grinned and pistoned his hips, slamming into her hard and deep.

"Oh, oh, do that, do that," she whimpered.

"You like that? Like to feel my cock deep inside your wet pussy?"

"Oh gods, yes, yes, please." She nodded, whimpering when he slowed down again.

"Like that? Or this?" he growled and picked up

the pace. She nodded again, scoring his back with her claws. His Bear roared, loving her scratches on his skin.

"Want more? Want me to make you come all over my cock? Want to feel my hot cum filling you up inside?"

Her fervent nod was all the answer he needed. Javier pressed his lips to hers in a new kiss, a desperate one with teeth and tongues warring with one another.

Bloody hell, she was feisty and incredible. Everything he ever wanted in a mate. And she was his mate, despite her refusal to acknowledge it, she was his and he was going to keep her.

"Gonna make you come soon, mate. All I need is your answer. Just say yes, say yes, yes," he growled, and she nodded in her fervor.

"Yes," she cried aloud.

Cradled between her soft, welcoming thighs, Javier rolled his hips, pushing all the way into her slick pussy. The second he felt her sheath tighten, he pushed the hair away from her neck and nuzzled her there, biting down the very same second, she screamed her pleasure.

Was it fair? No. But wasn't there a saying about all being fair in love and war? This was the battle of

Javi's life. His mate was everything to him, and he was going to show her she was right in saying yes. Starting right now.

His animal roared inside his head as he came inside of her and swallowed down her blood. He licked her neck, sealing the wound, and tried to control his breathing. He'd claimed her. She was his now.

Mate.

Chapter Nine

Hours later, Pamela woke up beside a naked and sexy as fuck male. She pulled her dress on quietly and tiptoed through the empty hallway. This was a walk of shame she had never quite done.

Shit. Fuck. Damn. He bit me!

Her she-Tiger chuffed and whined. The stupid animal wanted her to stay, to go back upstairs and snuggle with the big, warm male.

Mate, her beast called mournfully, but she shushed the creature.

How could she be so dumb? Sure, she'd been down for a little nooky, but he bit her. He marked her without her consent. The bastard.

Not true.

Fine—in his defense, Javier—*omfg how hot was his name? Eek! Ahem, be cool, girl, damn*—Javier had asked her to say yes. And she did. Pam had said yes—more like screamed it, but she didn't mean it.

For fuck's sake, he was holding her orgasm hostage! What was she supposed to say? Thank the gods he'd fallen into a heavy sleep—almost like he'd gone into hibernation—and she was able to get away. She had to admit, her curiosity was piqued. He smelled like Bear, but not like Brayden. He was different, somehow.

It didn't matter. He was none of her business.

Mate, the she-Cat pushed.

No. We have to go home. We have to take care of our cub.

The reminder of Paulie waiting for them back home was the only reason her Cat was allowing her to leave. Which was fine with Pam—if only she could make it out of the house without being seen. Tiptoeing through the dark with her heels in her hands and her hair and dress hopelessly mussed, she almost got away Scott free when she heard someone calling her name.

"Pamela Brown. Is that you sneaking around my house?"

Shit.

Pam turned around and smiled at Uncle Uzzi's knowing stare as the older Witch looked at her from head to bare toes.

"I see you had a good time?"

"Um, yeah, about that," she hedged, grasping for a way to apologize. "Uh, Elissa wanted me to thank you for inviting the Maverick Pride to participate—"

"Oh, my dear, please don't stand on ceremony with me," Uncle Uzzi took her arm and led her through a door to a corner of the kitchen where only a few staff remained to assist with the cleaning. "Now, you look like I did the first night I snuck home after meeting my liebling. We spent the night at a grand Witch ball, under the stars and making love. It was the best night of my life. But what I do not understand is why are you sneaking away? Did he hurt you?" Uncle Uzzi's blue eyes sparked at the suggestion.

"What? No!" Pamela replied, aghast at Uncle Uzzi's forthright manner—though she was not really surprised.

The man was known for his downright brutally honest approach to sex and mating. She appreciated that. Uzzi was a *no holds barred* kinda guy, which normally Pamela could get behind. Especially when someone else was in the hot seat.

"Um, it was fine. He was fine. Perfect gentleman," she said.

"Fine? Ugh, my dear, don't be boring. Be honest, you can talk to Uncle Uzzi, tell me everything," he said, popping a tiny bear cookie into his mouth that oddly enough reminded her of Javier.

"Okay, you got me. Javier was incredible, but there was a mistake. It was just for tonight, but well, he bit me," she whispered the last part.

"What? And you didn't want that? I swear I will zap *osito* right in the buttocks for forgetting his manners, my dear. A claiming bite, you say? And your Tiger allowed it?"

"Yes, my Tiger allowed it. And I guess I did to. I am just confused, Uncle Uzzi—" Pam stopped and cocked her head to the side. "*Osito?*"

"A nickname Javi had had since he was a cub," he informed her. "Javier Auberon is the best of men, but if he forced you into this, Pamela, I will do everything I can to try to change the outcome—"

"No! Uncle Uzzi, the truth is, he did not force me into anything. He's my mate," Pamela confessed, and the statement shocked even her. "I just need time. Please, Uncle Uzzi."

She looked up as the sound of a roar reverberated

in the mansion, followed by a crash, and thudding footsteps. Javier ran into the kitchen, looking more Bear than man, and Uncle Uzzi stepped in front of Pamela, who was stunned at the possessive display.

"Javier! Stop it right now," the older Witch commanded, and the half-man half-Bear Javi seemed to immediately calm down.

"Mate," he said in a calmer voice and looked back and forth from Pamela to the older Witch, his fur and claws receding. "Where did you go? Why did you leave? What happened, kitten?"

"Javi, there has been a mistake—"

"No. We are not a mistake. You are my mate," he insisted.

"Javi, let the woman breathe," Uncle Uzzi demanded, and Pamela was grateful for his intervention.

She wasn't sure she could resist Javi looking so handsomely disheveled, and smelling so good, like pine forests, mountain air, and the combination of their animals' fur. Just thinking about it sent tendrils of sensation hurtling throughout her body.

Pamela had to be honest with herself. She'd gone into heat almost instantly after just meeting the man. She'd fucked him like she couldn't survive without his cum. And here he was, larger than life, and wanting more.

Who did that? No guy she had ever been with.

Shit. Of course, she was confused. He'd made love to her like a god, and damn it, she had never felt so good before.

"Look, I suggest you go home, think about things Pamela—" Uzzi was saying, but Javi stepped forward, his dark eyes focused on her as his lips quirked into a grin.

"Pamela?" he repeated and smiled, saying her name a second time in his softly accented voice.

"Pamela. Yes, it fits. A beautiful name for a beautiful mate."

"Dear gods, Javier, didn't you ask the woman her name before you stuck your dick in her?" Uncle Uzzi shouted and bopped the Bear Shifter on the nose with a rolling pin, shaking his head.

The old Witch pointed his hand, zapping the male with blue sparking magic right on his naked chest when Javi reached for Pam. She winced at his discomfort but appreciated Uzzi's gesture. If that bear touched her, she would melt at his feet.

"Back off, *osito*. I can still kick your ass, you know."

"But—"

"No, butts. Pamela, go on home, and I will deal with Javi here, but be prepared. The fact is, he did claim you, and we have things to discuss. Make some time tomorrow to meet with us," instructed Uncle Uzzi.

"Okay," Pamela said, and her eyes filled with tears as warring thoughts and feelings churned like a twister inside her mind.

Confusion was the strongest, and she had to agree with Uncle Uzzi, she needed some time. Her eyes met Javier's once before she turned to leave. The hurt on his face was painful to witness, and she hated she was the one to cause it.

What else could she do, though?

This was supposed to be a one night only kinda thing. One night of *naughty* for all the other nights of being boringly *nice*.

Pamela just was not cut out for being a mate. She had a son to take care of and was only just finding herself and her place in the Pride. She didn't need a man to come into her life and mess it all up now.

"*Flaming fart balls,*" she muttered, and turned onto the highway to head back to Maverick Point.

No. She was not going to meet with Javier again. He was too tempting, and she wasn't strong enough to say no a second time.

Damn. Damn. DAMN.

Pamela's Tiger whined while she silently cried after turning off the radio for the entire trip back home. All those Christmas carols were making her feel worse. Why did she have to go and meet her mate now?

If only she were worthy of him.

Chapter Ten

Javier nursed his cup of coffee and waited for Uncle Uzzi to join him in the sitting room of the enormous penthouse suite he rented looking over Central Park. The old Witch had accompanied Javi back to New York City last night, though he was certain the old man had at least gotten some sleep, whereas all Javi did was roam the cold streets alone.

There was nothing quite like New York at Christmastime. The city was a magical place, but during December, it practically hummed with energy.

Uzzi had left him some pretty specific instruc-tions late that night, and Javier had followed. He was checked out of his room and had alerted his storage company to get all his belongings packed and ready at a moment's notice.

Anyone else would have been told to fuck off, but not Javier Auberon. When he said jump, smart people asked how high. It was one of the benefits of being wealthy and having a good reputation. Javi not only tipped well, but he tended to hire employees on the go.

If he met someone while traveling who was efficient, pleasant, and seemed like good people, Javier would offer a place at *Auberon Industries*. The salaries his company offered were competitive, and his healthcare packages unbeatable. Healthy staff meant productive staff. It was the first rule of running a sound business.

But his mind was not on his company at that moment. Javi's brain kept going over what had occurred between himself and the beautiful Pamela. It had been the best night of his life, but she left.

Uncle Uzzi had a shit ton to say to Javier about his not so brilliant plan to sex his way into Pamela's heart. He'd been thinking with his dick, and not his brain—but it did not matter in the least to Javier. He'd claimed the tender beauty as his own and had no intentions of tucking tail and running away.

He hated to argue with his uncle, but there was

no way he would abandon her. He had nothing to do and nowhere else to be. His mate was his one and final destination.

"There, that is better," Uzzi walked into the room, buttoning his sharp wool coat and tossing a long red scarf around his neck.

He'd always been a snazzy dresser, and Javi nodded his approval. Uzzi smiled sadly at him, and his Bear bellowed mournfully inside. The old Witch knew he was hurting too much to feel anything other than pain. His beast was positively desperate to track down his mate.

She belonged with him. Didn't she see that?

Bloody hell.

How had he fucked up so completely? Didn't even get her name until Uncle Uzzi had told it to him. He'd behaved like an animal, and he was deeply ashamed of himself. Javier should've treated her gently. Gotten to know her better first. Well, the least he should've done was ask her name before he had his face buried between her legs.

Memories of their night together plagued him for the past twelve hours, and Javi missed her with an ache he could not describe. It was like losing a limb. He felt her absence keenly. She was already bonded to him and his Bear.

Now that he'd had a taste of heaven, Javi wanted more. He wanted her with a hunger he'd never felt. Needed to be close to her, to know she was with him.

Fuck, was he crazy? To want someone all the time? He knew it was only going to get worse before it got better. Pamela Brown was his soulmate, his other half, the only woman in the world who spoke to him and his Bear, but he had tried to win her over with sex, and now he would have to earn her trust.

"Javi, focus. Hank, my driver, is here," Uncle Uzzi snapped his fingers in his face, and Javi followed him out the door and into the elevator like the lovesick fool he was.

"Uncle Uzzi, please, help me win Pamela's trust and, more importantly, her heart," Javier said, and wiped a hand over his face.

The city lights faded away in the face of his desperation, and Javier ignored the sounds of the crowds and honking horns around them.

"In time, Javi."

He dropped into the backseat with Uzzi as Hank pulled out onto the highway, the engine of the sleek limo purring gently, reminding him of his little wild cat.

Fuck, I miss her.

"There is no time. I have to get her back. Tell me how, please," he begged.

"Javier, I love you dearly, but you know it isn't polite to stick your dick in a woman before you explain a few things first," Uncle Uzzi said, his sapphire gaze sparking mad as it landed on Javi.

"Uncle Uzzi, please be respectful. She is my mate," he moaned.

"Who me, disrespectful? Dear boy, you are the one who took his dick, stuck it in the woman—whose name you did not bother to get—exploiting her heat cycle for your own gain. Then, let's see, you bit her neck. Claiming her for your Bear, and you expected her to jump for joy. Does that sum it up? *Stupido!*" Uzzi zapped him and Javi clenched his teeth. Fuck, but he deserved it.

"I fucked up. I know. But I love her—"

"Did you ever think she had a reason for saying no, *osito*? Ever consider there was something in her past she needed to confront first?"

Fuck.

No. To be honest, Javier had not considered anything like it. He started to panic, wondering what she had in her past that would make her deny her fated mate. Oh shit. Oh fuck. What could it be?

Stupid impatient motherfucker.

"What do you mean, Uncle Uzzi? Is it another man? She did not wear a mating mark, I'd have sensed it, but if she was involved, I'll, I'll—"

Tear the motherfucker limb for limb, his unhelpful bear supplied.

"Calm your fur, *osito*. There has been no boyfriend for the last year or so. Though there is someone important in her life. Just be patient with her. Not everyone has had your charmed life," he said, drumming his fingers on his knee before he continued.

"Who is he?" Javier growled, his voice deep with his Bear.

If it was a Shifter, Javi would issue a formal challenge for the right to pursue his mate. Pamela was not a possession, but fuck yes, he wanted to possess her. It was a Shifter thing. He would always celebrate her independence, as long as he could be there when she needed him. Her comfort and happiness were everything to him. If there was a man, Javier would happily prove he was the better of the two. No matter what it took.

"Pamela has had a rough time of it, but thanks to her friends and the members of her Pride, she has really made incredible strides for a better life for herself—and for *her son.*"

"What? Did you say—son?"

Javier couldn't stop the growl that followed the word. It wasn't that he didn't like children, on the contrary, but he never imagined his mate would already have a child. Strange feelings rose inside him. He'd expected jealousy and maybe anger, but all he got was, well, curiosity. A deep, burning need to meet the boy, to make sure he was alright.

A son. She has a son. We have a son.

"Whose child is it?"

"He is her child, *osito*. And don't act like a possessive asshole in heat, Javi. Paulie is one of the sweetest little Tiger cubs I have ever met," Uncle Uzzi said, and his eyes glowed at the mention of the young boy.

"Of course, I did not mean it that way. I love kids, and my Bear is a little possessive right now. He is already calling the boy ours," he explained.

"Good. Cause that is non-negotiable. Paulie is part of the deal."

"Yes. As he should be, a little prince," he murmured, already picturing the things he would show the boy with his mother's permission, of course. "My Bear wants young, and any cub of Pamela's is my own as well, if she will have me," Javier said, wishing with everything inside him that he could make it so. His Bear chuffed softly, already staking his claim on the unseen child.

Amazing that the second Uncle Uzzi had mentioned a cub, his Bear had seemed to take the idea of the cub as his own. The only thing that bothered him was thinking of another male's hands on his Pamela. Idiot. She was not a virgin when they met, and neither was he. He had no right to expect that, and Javi scolded the Bear. He loved the woman as she was, it did not matter how she got there. Only that it made her stronger, happier, better—*simply perfect for him in every way.*

"So, let's talk about homes. You said you were moving to the states. Now, Maverick Point, New Jersey, is quite the ideal little town. Here, I printed some pictures for you of properties, and this is the number for a local real estate agent."

Uncle Uzzi handed him a red folder and Javi grinned at the man. Brilliant. This was exactly what he needed—a den, a place to plant roots, to prove he was serious about his commitment. Pamela needed her Pride, so he would move to where they lived.

"Uncle Uzzi, you are a genius."

"I know, *osito,*" the old Witch said calmly. "Now, why don't you find a home that would be suitable for a family—your family. That is, if you're lucky,"

Uzzi finished, and the confounded man shook his head as if he had his doubts.

No matter. Uncle Uzzi could bet against him, but Javier was not losing her. He made a vow right then and there to do anything he could to make Pamela see that he was the only man for her.

Whatever happened in her past, it was just that. He was sorry she had been hurt, wished like hell he could have stopped it. But the best he could do now was to ensure Pamela and her sweet cub were safe from here on out.

Love. Mate. Mine. Cub.

His Bear chuffed and pawed at the ground inside the metaphysical plane where he waited to be freed. Yes, they would be home soon, then he would let him out for a bit.

I am going to love you so much, Pamela Brown. You and Paulie. Starting now. And I will prove myself to you, my naughty little minx.

You're the only thing on my list this year, querida. Naughty or nice, here I come.

Chapter Eleven

"Cut It Out, can I help you?" Pamela answered the phone.

It seemed to be ringing off the hook, but that was the holidays for you. She grabbed a sheet of paper and a pen and took down the message before checking the rest of her schedule.

"Gretchen? Your six o'clock canceled," she called out to her boss.

"Really? Good, I need to get off my feet," her pregnant boss replied.

She rubbed her swollen tummy and stretched. Her belly was looking quite low. Pam and Marion, the other stylist, and a good friend, exchanged concerned looks. If Marion was worried about her, then that was cause for alarm, since the man was a huge proponent of tough love.

Hmmm. Gretchen needed to rest more, carrying a Shifter cub was not at all easy. Especially since Gretchen was new to the whole Shifter thing, having undergone the *Puspa* only months ago. All those physical and physiological changes were bound to catch up with her at some point.

"Say, why don't you go home and put your feet up? Marion and I will stay and take care of things till closing," Pamela said, and Marion nodded his agreement.

"No, I couldn't leave you guys here—"

"Boss lady, are you for real? Girrrl, it's only an hour till closing. Me and girlfriend here got this, besides I have to put some highlights back in Miss Thang's head after work any who," he added, and winked at Pamela.

"Really? You decided to put some back after all?" Gretchen asked, and Pam could tell she was excited.

After years of mistreating her hair, Pamela had taken all the bleach out and let her brown locks grow in. But part of her affirmation and growth meant owning who she was, and Pamela loved highlights. She was finished letting the past control her present.

"Yes, Marion said he would do them. I hope that's okay—"

"*Ermagerd, yesss!* What? I am so excited for you," Gretchen said and started tearing up again. Darn pregnancy hormones.

"Woman, get your ass home and tell your man you need a foot rub *stat*," Marion demanded, already prepping his station and getting foils out for Pam's hair.

"Word, I am texting Reg right now," Gretchen said, then turned to ask one more time. "You sure?"

"Yes," Pamela and Marion both said together.

They spent the next forty minutes putting highlights in Pamela's hair, giggling, and making innuendos about how she's spent the night at the ball.

"Come on, Pamela, Gretchen will be staring at the same dick—no offense honey we know Reg is hot—and I have not seen one in the flesh in ages, now tell us the deets," Marion snapped.

"I don't know what you are talking about, Mar," she said primly.

"That is some serious *toro excretio*, Miss Thang. And I mean like whopping Cretan Bull-sized shit, *er*, shiznit—don't look flabbergasted, read some Homer, *peasant*," he said, and sniffed delicately while the girls busted out laughing.

"Look, I don't kiss and tell, but if you two must know—"

"Damn straight, we do," Gretch inserted.

"I met someone," Pamela said, downplaying her encounter with Javier.

The sound of a familiar truck pulled up, and Gretchen lit up like a lightbulb at the sight of her mate. Foils and all, Pamela stood up and practically carried her happily mated—*and very, very pregnant*—boss outside into the open arms of her man. Reg nodded and scooped up his woman, ready to take her to their new house.

"See ya later, boss lady!"

Pamela waved the couple off and looked up at the pinkish white sky. Looked like they were in for more snow, but that was okay with her. She was a sucker for everything Christmassy, and besides, Paulie loved to play in the fluffy white stuff.

"Okay, Pam, you have ten more minutes, rinse, tone, and condition. Now, come on, Mrs. Jones, let's go get you settled," Marion said in a sing-song voice to his client.

Pamela giggled, not even minding that she looked like a nut job with multicolored squares of foil all over her head. She only had one more client, but not until later that evening. Right then, she had to prep the nail stations for the following day. Everyone wanted to get their nails done for the upcoming holidays. They asked for everything from snowmen to Santa hats, candy canes and more.

Gretchen had gone into order mode with triple her usual supplies, but they'd been so busy all week, there'd been no time to set them up. Luckily, the she-Tiger had hired two new nail techs, and Pamela only had to worry about doing hair, which she liked infinitely better than nails.

Marion was telling Mrs. Jones a story that had the older woman blushing, and Pamela giggled. She loved this job. The people were so much fun to work with and Gretchen most of all. She had proven a truly gifted instructor, taking it upon himself to show her the ins and outs of cutting hair.

She still had to take the final test for dying hair to be fully licensed in the state of New Jersey, but she was more than ready. The timer for her hair went off, and Pamela removed the foils, rinsed out the bleach. Then she toned it and added a deep Moroccan oil treatment. By the time her conditioning masque—*a necessary step for dyed hair*—was finished, she had restocked the nail stations and sanitized all the equipment.

"Want me to dry you while Mrs. Jones' dye is still working its magic?" Marion asked.

"Nah, I'll be fine. I have to run these to the dumpster."

"Alrighty," Marion replied.

It was warm in the store, and Pam had been wearing a sporty little skort and a long-sleeved crop top to work, and a pair of comfy Converse on her feet. She was humming to herself when she stepped outside, but the sound stopped as she shivered against the sudden blast of wintry wind.

It wasn't the cold that had her back up, it was the scent that had accompanied said breeze. Dank and musty, not at all pleasant. Pamela turned to see a familiar, and unwelcomed face standing beside the dumpster where she was just about to place the plastic bag in her hand.

"'Bout time you got your fat ass out here," the Hyena barked. "Say you put on some weight, didn't you? Oh well, Alpha is looking to party. Let's go."

"What did you say to me?" she asked, stunned at this jerk's audacity.

"Look, bitch. Blake promised us easy access to his harem, and you were the prize most coveted. I am calling in the favors we did for that asshole. Now, let's go."

"I don't think so—"

The Hyena snarled, spitting on the floor as he stalked her until she almost had to back up a step to avoid his touch.

"Don't you dare touch me," she hissed, not liking how he was crowding her.

She did not want to take that step backwards, but his rank breath and creepy grin brought back horrible memories. Then suddenly, Pamela did not have to move at all—the Hyena male was making gurgling noises. His whole body hovered in the air. His choking was replaced by the sound of a deep, rumbling growl that filled the entire alley behind *Cut It Out*.

Pamela gasped. Stunned, she looked around the Hyena, who was choking and fighting against a huge hand the skinny fucker had no hope of removing. In fact, he was turning an unhealthy shade of blue, but Pamela was not concerned for his lack of oxygen. She wanted to see who her rescuer was.

"Javi!" She gasped. "What are you—"

The words died on her lips as she took in the expression of pure fury on Javier Auberon's handsome face. His eyes had bled to the glittering black of his Bear and fur dusted his cheeks as he barely held on to his skin. Her body reacted predictably to his dominant display, and she shivered uncontrollably against another blast of cold wind.

Javier was the one man she didn't expect to run in to in the alley behind her job. Even though Uncle Uzzi said to expect them today, but Pamela didn't know he meant like today *today*.

"Do you know this man?" he asked, his voice thick with his Bear and showing more traces of his heritage.

She'd been texting Uncle Uzzi all day, and the man had shared some photos of young Javi and his brother, Gabriel. He was born in Quito, Ecuador, and his brother still lived there, having taken over the role of Alpha in their small family unit. It was all so new to her, and she enjoyed the hints she'd gleaned off the old Witch of Javi's life. The best would be revealed to her by the man himself.

Maybe. If he stuck around after this. And if I do.

"Unfortunately, I do," she muttered. "But he is not welcome here. Go tell your Alpha that if he is looking to cash in on some debt from Blake, he'll have to follow that jerk to Hell to get it."

"And if you come looking for Pamela again, know that she has friends now, *mutt*. You heard her. Get lost, and forget this town," growled Javier, before tossing him halfway down the alley with one shove.

Pamela had to admit, that felt damn good. Telling off that creep, having Javi at her back, standing her ground, and letting him know she would not be pushed around. Yeah, it felt really good. She waited while the Hyena scrambled to run away, and she bit back a laugh as he skidded on some ice and yelped when he heard Javi snarl angrily.

"Move faster," he told the terrified Hyena.

"That was awesome," Pamela whispered, and Javi turned his head to look at her.

"Hello, Pamela," he said, his Bearish growl rumbling through her.

Christ, he was sexy. Pamela raked him with her gaze, and her body warmed with the memory of how well he'd loved her the night before. What was she going to do about him? His smoldering good looks were red carpet worthy, and here she was looking like some sort of cheerleader reject with frozen hair.

"So are you gonna show me where you work?" he asked in that same, deep, husky voice that had whispered the most deliciously naughty things in her ears just the night before.

"Um, yep, sure. Oh, um, hi," she replied, turning her back on him and hurrying into the salon through the back door. "So, what are you doing here? Where is Uncle Uzzi?"

"He had an appointment, and I thought maybe we could talk alone. Is that alright? Will you talk with me?" he asked, and his black eyes twinkled mischievously.

"I can't. I'm working. Actually, I have an appointment with a new client who should be here any minute—"

"Actually, he is here now." Javi smiled, and yep, there went her panties.

Jingle all the way.

Chapter Twelve

"Y our appointment is with me," Javier told her, and she stumbled, spinning around too quickly with her wet-soled Converse on the polished floor.

"Easy, *querida*," he whispered, steadying her with his hands. He let go when she pushed on them. And right away, she missed his touch.

Sad chuff.

Zip it furball.

She ignored her Tiger's annoyed hiss and crossed her arms. Why did he do that? She needed answers, but things got confused when he touched her. No, absolutely no touching until he spilled the beans.

"So, you're J.A. who needed the last possible appointment? What you're like stalking me now?"

Pamela narrowed her eyes at him, though she was really more flattered than she was annoyed at him. Javi's bronzed cheeks burned a deep crimson color as he rubbed the back of his neck while he tried to find an explanation.

"Okay, I admit it. I wanted to see you without you getting all tense, and I thought this would be a good solution. So, yes, J.A. is for Javier Auberon. And while stalker is not a nice word, I guess I am busted."

Then he did it again—*naughty Bear*. He gave her a crooked, panty-melting grin, the kind mothers warned their daughters about the world over. But it was too late. Javier Auberon was in Maverick Point, at Pamela's place of work, and her heart was going berserk.

Bum bum. Bum bum. Bum bum.

"I hope you do not take this the wrong way, but it is nice to formally meet you, Pamela Brown," he added, and she found herself blushing furiously.

Their first meeting had been a headlong rush into *naughty land* with the sounds of the holidays buzzing in the background. Last night had been the best night of her life, from a purely physical stand-point of course—only he was right. She never told him her name.

Gulp.

His dark eyes glittered like one of those seven dollar bars of chocolate she always wanted to try but couldn't rationalize splurging when there were other things she needed to buy with her hard earned cash. Was Javi like that, she wondered.

Was he too rich for her blood? Too expensive to take a chance on. And she wasn't talking about monetarily, she was talking about her heart. Could Pamela really afford to lose even one inch of that muscle to a man? Everything inside of her screamed yes, but she was still wary.

Dangerous man. Sexy, charming, protective Bear.

"Okay, Mrs. Jones, you are almost dry," Marion said loudly, while taking covert glances at Javier. He made an OMG face and gave Pam a big thumbs up on the not so sly.

Her cheeks heated, and Pamela licked her lips, tucking her wet hair behind her ears. She did not even want to think about what she looked like.

"I like what you did with the highlights," he murmured before turning to greet her co-worker. "Hello there, I'm Javi."

"Yes, you are a hottie," Marion said and winked.

"No, it's Javi—oh, I see, well, thank you for the compliment," Javier said, cocking his head to the side adorably.

The man was just too hot for words, as Marion had said. But, oh my—damn, was he blushing? He was embarrassed by the attention! Now, that was unusual. She'd have expected a man like that to have an ego the size of a mountain. It was nice to know he didn't.

Her Tiger chuffed and purred. The animal ready to go belly up to beg for pets and cuddles. Had she no shame? Sigh. Pamela closed her eyes and tried to rein in her beast, but she was pulled pretty thin, what with trying to calm her ovaries and all.

"Who are you?" Mrs. Jones asked.

"I'm Javi, ma'am."

"Well, Javi, I'm married, but oooh, if I were twenty years younger this would be a different conversation, *you little stud muffin,*" Mrs. Jones said, and Marion and Javi both chuckled loudly.

"Okay, ready? Sit down," Pamela said, irrationally jealous of the old lady.

Oh hell. This was ridiculous. She needed psychiatric help or something. Pamela shook her head and recalled the appointment book J.A. had asked for a pedicure. Fine. She could do that. She pointed to one of the luxury pedicure chairs.

"Uh, I thought maybe a trim?" he eyed the chair doubtfully.

Pamela raised an eyebrow, seizing her chance to really test him. That and there was no way she was cutting that luscious head of hair. She loved his thick, glossy locks and the way they fell over his forehead in sexy disarray.

"Sorry, J.A. I am not a full stylist yet, and my supervising manager had to leave early. So, if you don't want me to give you a pedicure, then I am afraid it is nothing. Bye-bye, see you never," she stated and pursed her lips.

"Okay, on second thought, I could use a little *TLC* in the foot department. Thank you, kitten," he replied and winked.

Great. Gorgeous and confident in his masculinity. The guy was a freaking gem. Pamela huffed out an annoyed breath. She had to admit, it shocked her that he was just going with this. Most men did not want to have their nails done, but Javier merely nodded and shrugged out of his stylish wool coat.

He hung the expensive garment on the hook beside the chair, and she noted his clothes were all cut to fit his large, muscular frame. There was no way they made regular clothes that big.

She cleared her throat, trying not to get hot and bothered by the way he bent over and untied his expensive looking Italian shoes. Next were his socks, red and green paisley—*nice and festive*—and she found herself wondering if he wore colorful socks as a sort of rebellion against conforming to what society deemed was proper masculine attire or just for comfort.

More worrisome were the designer labels she could read from this distance, and biting her lower lip, she looked down nervously at her own beat up sneakers. Just more proof she and Javi were worlds apart. It was obvious he had money. *Like tons of it.*

But she'd guessed that already from his easy grace, excellent manners, and stylish clothing. Even the cadence with which he spoke shouted higher education and a fancy upbringing. She cleared her throat. That line of thinking only made her doubt herself, and Pamela was done with negativity in her life.

Javi was here, and he was trying to get to know her. She should try to reserve her judgement for later—after she told him the truth about her past. If Prince Charming was still interested after her warts were revealed, then they might have a fighting chance at making this thing work. Hope was a precious thing, so fragile and easily discouraged.

Could she trust him with hers? Pamela wanted to. She really did. She was trying to be more optimistic, but taking chances was scary as hell. After all, it was not just herself she was risking. It was Paulie's life too.

This was hard, she realized. Difficult and frightening as fuck, but she was not a weakling. Pamela was a Tiger. She just had to remember that while she got to work laying out the various scrubs, oils, lotions, and tools she would need for the job.

"Did you want any polish?" she asked, with a little bit of cheek.

Javi raised an eyebrow and grinned, that patented panty-melting one she was starting to love. Then, the beast just shook his head, sending his wavy locks cascading over his forehead.

Holy hotness. She bit back her moan and set his feet—*oh boy, he had nice feet too.* The Fates really were not playing fair. She was a sucker for a guy who took care of himself, and Javi had that distinction.

He watched her with his dark, unwavering gaze, and she felt goosebumps break out along her skin. There was no doubt about it, Pamela had seriously underestimated how intimate this setup was. Usually, she gave pedicures to little old ladies and noisy teenagers, but Javier Auberon was neither.

Determined to keep her cool, she straddled the rolling stool, grateful for her skort since she had to part her legs in order to lean over to roll up his jeans. She groaned softly as his mountain fresh male musk invaded her nostrils. The scent so tempting, it made her Tiger want to roll around in it, in him.

Prrrrrrrrr.

Her stomach clenched and she damn near salivated when she found herself mere inches away from the hardness hidden beneath the expensive denim as she ran her nails up his muscular calves, securing his pants at his knees. Javier's eyes flashed like black glass, his Bear peeking out at her, and she wanted to smirk, but this was affecting her as well.

What she wouldn't give to rip those jeans off of him right now! Holy hell. A wave of pure need washed over her, but Pam was a professional. She'd thought her heat had come and gone after they'd made love countless times last night, but obviously her inner kitty wanted more of the big bad Bear.

"That feels nice, *querida*," he murmured as she started the process of giving the sexy bear a pedicure.

He had nice feet, she'd noted that already. And a small, submissive part of her was completely turned on as she applied a little soap and scrub to her hands, then rubbed each one all the way up his calves. Rinse and repeat. Javi moaned and growled.

His eyes heated as she massaged his legs and hit his arches just right. When she started filing his already trimmed and cleaned nails, he hazarded a question. Thank fuck, she was so tense she was ready to snap.

"I'd like to take you out for dinner, after this. If you'd like?" he asked.

"I'm sorry," she began automatically. Her eyes narrowed before she told him the truth about why. Pamela was not free to just make plans at the drop of a hat like other women. She had responsibilities.

"I see," he mumbled, sounding disappointed. She exhaled and grabbed some lotion, applying it to his heels and ankles, where the skin was rougher.

"The reason I can't go is that I have to pick up my son when I am finished here," she explained, and waited for his reaction.

Her heart squeezed in her chest as the seconds ticked by. She was certain now that she had used the right ammunition to send the Bear running. Pulling on her inner reserves of strength, Pamela lifted her gaze to his, ready for his anger or revulsion, but the man was just grinning at her. His joy was almost tangible.

"Can I go with you? I can't wait to meet little Paulie, Uncle Uzzi told me all about him. In fact, I took the liberty of getting him a small gift for the holidays," he said, and Pamela was stunned.

There was nothing pre-calculated about this, nothing dishonest or her Tiger would know. The animal had gotten very good at sniffing out bullshit over the past year. But with Javi she only smelled good intentions and warmth. He seemed genuinely excited.

"Check this out," he told her and reached over to grab something from the pocket of his coat.

She watched in complete surprise as he pulled out a tiny wooden llama. The smile on his face was so real, it made her grin, too. The gesture alone touched something inside of Pamela, and she couldn't help but sigh a little.

Sweet, thoughtful, sexy Bear.

"It's so cool," she said, taking it when he offered. "But that must be an heirloom or something. The detail is extraordinary, and the wood seems aged—"

"Well, my grandfather hand-carved this for me when I was a boy," he explained. "I named him Tito, which is what I called my *abuelito* back then. Anyway, Tito has been neglected for a long time now. He needs someone to take care of him, and I thought Paulie might like to do that."

"Oh Javi, that's really sweet," she said, and he just

shrugged, ducking his head as if uncomfortable with the praise.

Bum bum. Bum bum. Bum bum.

Her heart melted a little bit more, as she watched him tuck the llama carefully back into his pocket. She hadn't answered him yet, but how could she refuse when he had something so precious to gift to her son? Pamela pulled the plug on the water in the basin leftover from his pedicure and hoped the sound would drown out the flood of emotions threatening to consume her.

This was really big. Huge. That llama was a cherished childhood toy, and Javier wanted to give it to her son—a boy who was fathered by another man. With Shifters, situations like that could go either way. A mate could just as easily reject offspring from prior relationships, but Javi seemed to do the opposite.

Hope welled up inside of her, but she was too afraid to let it take flight. Could he be telling the truth? Did he really not mind the fact that she had a son?

"Pamela, look at me," he said as she rolled his pant legs down. She met his eyes reluctantly.

"Hear the truth in my voice, kitten," he whispered. "The second Uncle Uzzi told me about Paulie, my Bear and I both decided he was ours. I want very much to meet him. I will not lie to you. Not now and not ever. The idea of other men being intimate with you makes my Bear very jealous," he said, and she heard his truth. She swallowed, confused. "But kitten, I swear on my life, I have nothing but good-will towards Paulie. He came from you, sweet cub, and I can hope that one day you will allow me to call him mine as well."

"Javier, I never had anyone around him. He never saw his father, and that man is gone. Killed by the Neta. He was evil and bad, and I was with him for a long time. He made me do things I am not proud of —" she confessed, swallowing her tears.

"No, querida, you have nothing to be sorry for," he murmured and took her hands, pulling her up until she was sitting on his lap.

It felt so good, wrapped in his big, strong arms, leaning on someone else for a change. Pamela slumped against him, allowing him to hold her weight, and the silly Bear growled and kissed her head as he hugged her to him.

"The past is the past, Pamela," he said, shushing her gently when she protested. "I know it seems soon, but I care for you, greatly. It is too early to say the words, but my Bear chooses you. *I* choose you and nothing you tell me will change my mind," he said, cupping her cheeks and holding her stare.

"I am not going anywhere, *querida*. You can't scare me with skeletons in your closet. We all have them. Now, I promise, I will do anything you want, go as slow as you want to, even if it kills me," he murmured, and she laughed. "When I say you are my fated mate, that means I will do whatever it takes to get to be the only man by your side, and Paulie's, for the rest of my life. I want you, Pamela. Only you. All of you. And I promise to be the man you need, *kitten*."

"Oh Javi," she whispered and smashed her lips to his.

She was too overwhelmed for words. But this was a place of business and with Marion and Mrs. Jones applauding, she figured she should knock it off. Pulling away from him was hard, but Javi seemed to know the struggle. He pressed his forehead to hers and breathed deep, rubbing her back with his large, warm hands.

She needed to do something, say anything, to break the tension. Hell, she was compelled to do so. So, she commented on one simple truth she'd been meaning to say.

"You know, you have really nice feet for a guy," she said, and Javi laughed.

"Thank you, querida. You have really nice everything," he growled softly, and her whole body seemed to vibrate in response.

"I am sorry, I can't help it," he apologized, but the heated look he gave her said he was anything but sorry.

"One moment, kitten."

She'd been trying to stand, but Javi's strong hands held her still for another moment. Pamela gasped as she felt the reason pulsing beneath her bottom. And there went her panties.

"Oh," she said in a rush of air.

The look on his face was hot enough to melt iron. His black eyes flashed and sent shockwaves of awareness flitting through her blood. Pamela swayed closer to the big, sexy man as if drawn by some unseen magnetic force.

"Whenever you touch me, it's like this. With you, I am in paradise," he told her, his voice so low, it was perfect for her sensitive ears, but also guaranteed no one else would hear. Good. She wanted this to be their moment.

"It was just a pedicure."

"It was so much more than that. I did not sleep a wink after you left last night."

"You didn't?"

"I couldn't. Not without you. You make love like a dream, querida, purring beneath me like a kitten, but scratching at my back like a wildcat. I want that again. I want you completely nude and writhing beneath my body while I take you in every way imaginable. I want to mark you again, and I want your bite, kitten. My Bear needs it. It's all I can think about," he said huskily.

"Javier—"

Hot damn.

The man was really messing with her inner peace. She shook her head and stood up, cleaning the station while he donned his socks and shoes. She tried to ignore his husky little whispers, and whispered words of praise, but it was difficult. He complimented her like no one ever had before. Even helped her clean and return the cart with the tools to the sanitizer.

By the time they finished, she was so turned on, Pamela seriously considered taking ten minutes to go to the restroom so she could make herself come. Just so she could function for the rest of her day. Not a bad idea, she mused and excused herself to the ladies' room. He would smell that on her though, so she was resolved to splash some ice cold water on her face, just to cool off—only Javier followed her into the small restroom.

"This is for employees only," she started, but his lips were already crashing into hers as he swallowed the rest of her words.

Oh fuck. The man stole her breath. Literally. Their kiss was so hot Pamela felt as though she was going to combust right there.

"I want you so badly, *querida,*" he groaned into her mouth, sucking on her upper lip while his hands made quick work of her skort and damp panties.

Their frantic movements caused her to knock over a box with the rest of the Christmas decorations onto the floor. Jingle bells, glittery garland, and an open box of silver tinsel went flying as his fingers delved between her legs.

"Oh fuck. Yes. I mean, what are you doing?" she hissed, as Javier dropped to his knees and nuzzled her nether lips apart with his nose and mouth.

He grabbed one thigh and lifted it, draping it over his shoulder while Pamela held onto the sink for support. She bit her fist to quell the sound of her lusty moan as his tongue swiped across her slit.

"I'm starving for you," he growled, spreading her

lips apart with his fingers. "Gonna eat this pretty pussy until your honey is dripping down my chin," he growled, and closed his mouth over her hot sex in an open-mouthed kiss that sent jolts of heat buzzing through her veins.

"Oh gods!"

"Javier. Say it. Tell me what you want. Say my name when you tell me, kitten," he growled and plunged into her heat with his tongue, licking her all the way to her clit and back again, then he stopped.

She looked down and saw he was waiting for her to speak. Pamela nodded her head. Fingers wound in his dark locks, she pushed him back between her thighs and answered him.

"Yes, I want you to kiss me, to lick me, to make me come with your mouth. Please, *Javierrrr*," she purred.

The sound turned to a groan as he suckled her needy sex with gusto, his growls and prehensile lips driving her insane. Someone turned up the sound system inside the shop and *Santa Claus is Comin' to Town* rang through the air.

He wasn't the only one coming, Pamela gasped.

Tension built inside her. Her stomach clenched and shivers raced up and down her body. Pamela drank in the sight of Javier and the *oh so naughty* things he was doing to her in the mirror behind them. His magnificent mouth was bringing her to heights she had never experienced.

Holy forking fart balls.

She hadn't felt this good in forever. She bit her hand, quivering uncontrollably as she came and came and came.

"Mine," he growled, lifting his head, his mouth and face glistening with the evidence of her pleasure.

Pamela had never seen anything as sexy as Javier covered in her juices. She grabbed him by the shirt and pulled him in for a long, hard kiss, wrapping her legs around his waist.

She needed him. Now.

Chapter Thirteen

nock-knock!

The sound of someone banging on the door wasn't enough to bring Javier down from the natural high he got licking and sucking on his mate's cinnamon honey flavored pussy. The naughty little noises she'd made as she rocked her hips against his face had his dick threatening to punch a hole through his jeans. And the way she'd grabbed him for a deep kiss after was so fucking hot.

"Pamela? It's Marion, um, I'm gonna go ahead and lock up. You can punch in the alarm code when you're ready to leave, okay? Girl, uh, you okay?"

"Yes, yes!" she cried out, but Javi was pretty damn certain that had everything to do with his shoving two fingers into her tight little pussy just then, and nothing at all to do with the other stylist's questions.

Good thing the man left when he did. Shit was about to get louder. Javier growled against Pamela's lips, having already lifted her off the floor with both legs around his waist. He unfastened his jeans, pushed them down, but paused a moment.

Last time they did this, it had been under the influence of her heat and his mating fever. This time, he wanted her full consent. Her body twitched, and he held her, confident in his ability to satisfy his lusty little kitten's appetites and his own. She pulled on his hair, rubbing her slick sex against the bar of his cock, and fuck, he almost lost it. Javier kissed her lips, pressing his forehead to hers and forcing her to pause.

"Please, Javi, need you," she whispered.

"I need you too, Pamela. But I want you to be sure it is me you want."

"Yes. You. Only you," she growled, her voice thick with her Tiger.

"Tell me what you want," he said.

"Fuck me, Javi. I want you to fuck me. Now."

Then he had no choice. He pressed the head of his cock into her, inch by inch, slowly, until she was full of him. They groaned in unison, and he thanked the Fates for matching him with this unparalleled female. Her tight heat squeezed him, and Javi had to fight for control.

"I am fucking you, kitten, only you, forever you," he growled, then he moved.

"Javi!" she said, repeating his name until it was nothing but a hoarse cry on her gorgeous lips.

"That's it, baby, come for me. Now, let go," he commanded, praising her through it all.

Javier sucked at her lips, savoring the residual honeyed taste they both shared. He fucked her in long, deep strokes, massaging her g-spot in slow, circular swirls of his hips. Fuck, her pussy clenched around him, and it felt like pure heaven. He could get lost in her, he realized, was positively drunk on her at this very moment.

Mine. Mine. MINE.

She was a deadly combination of brains, beauty, body, and compassion. Pamela Brown owned him, body, mind, soul, and heart. Yes, she ruled that particular organ. Hell, he would gladly rip the thing from his chest for her. He would do anything and everything she wanted. Always.

His mate caught his mouth in a deep kiss, arching against him and squeezing him tight. Her desire spurred him on, and he growled as he kissed the hell out of her. Just knowing they were more than compatible in this way was enough to make him believe their future was bright indeed.

The kiss turned urgent, and it wasn't long before he was withdrawing his cock and slamming back home, balls deep inside of her. Sex with his mate was explosive, beyond anything he'd ever felt, but he wanted more. He wanted it all.

"I'm coming," she moaned, clutching his shoulders in her pleasure. Fuck, Javi had no choice but to come with her, filling her with his seed so deep she would never be rid of his scent.

Mine.

Pride filled him as her body pulsated around him, and he drew out her orgasm with slow, tiny strokes. He had her body, but it was not enough.

Javier wanted her love. He wanted to be branded by her, to proudly wear her mating mark on his skin. He wanted her belly full of his cubs. He wanted to be a father to her son, and a mate to her for all time. She was his.

He just had to convince her.

After they'd straightened their clothing and closed up the salon, Javier walked Pamela to his Mercedes. Uncle Uzzi had very thoughtfully had his car and other things driven down to the South

Jersey town before they'd even started their own drive.

The streets were dusted with snow, but the sidewalks were all neatly shoveled, making it look like a picture perfect portrayal of suburban life.

Multi-colored twinkle lights and wreaths bearing big red bows decorated every doorway. Maverick Point was the epitome of a quaint American town, and he'd felt at home the second he'd arrived.

"Where are we going?" Pamela asked.

"Don't you have to get Paulie?"

"Actually, I have some time. He's with the Nari. She said she would watch him so I could do some Christmas shopping," she told him and blushed, tucking a strand of hair into the messy bun she made on top of her head.

So cute, he thought and smiled indulgently.

"Wonderful. I would love to go with you," he said.

"Okay, good. The shopping center is this way," she said and gave him directions.

He enjoyed the drive through town—with Pamela beside him, how could he not? Maverick Point was a very nice place, he deduced. Close enough to the city to be useful if business called him in, but far enough so his Bear would never feel crowded.

Javi was shocked when the directions took them past a large home with a pale-yellow stucco and sand colored stone exterior. He was about to confess something, but Pamela's sad gasp had him stopping short.

"What is it?"

"Oh no," she moaned. "They took down the 'for sale' sign on my house!"

"Your house?"

"Well, no. It was my dream house," she said, embarrassment making her cheeks grow pink and her scent flare inside the small car.

Grrrr.

"Does it upset you it was bought?" he asked, genuinely interested.

"Well, I mean, I had my eye on it since they built this place about a year ago. Not that I could afford it on my salary, but I have it taped on my vision board. I guess I've had dreams of living in it. I know it's silly, but anyway, I hope it got sold to a good family," she sighed.

"I am sure it did," he nodded. "So, what is on Paulie's Christmas list?" Javier changed the subject. Some things were better left alone, he figured. While others made for interesting thinking.

"He's a really great boy. Sweet and caring, he

loves playing with the other kids in the Pride, now that the Neta has cubs, his mate made it her business to organize little get togethers for the children of everyone in the Pride. It's meant the world to Paulie. I want this Christmas to be a good one for him. He doesn't ask for a lot, but I want to give him the world."

Pamela beamed with pride as she described her son and all his adventures. Reciting the things he wanted for Christmas to Javier, who nodded excitedly. Buying toys seemed like a lot of fun.

"I can't wait to meet him," he said and opened the door for her as they arrived at the large and crowded mega store.

After an hour of strolling around, munching on popcorn, and filling the shopping cart despite her protests, Javier smiled happily as the cashier rang them up.

"I don't want you to think I asked you to come along to make you pay—"

"Hey," he told her, and kissed her lips. He meant it to be a simple, reassuring peck, but he moaned softly when she immediately responded to the small caress, leaning into him, and kissing him back.

"We are mates. I can feel your emotions through our bond, even though it is new, *querida*. I know you love Paulie so much it hurts. A young, innocent boy deserves to have a good Christmas. Let me do this for you," he begged.

"You really want to get to know my cub, even though his father was a bastard?" she whispered her question, and he saw the pain and doubt in her face.

Fuck, that hurt. He wanted to dig that fucker's grave up so he could kill him all over again.

"Pamela, I promise you, I would never judge your son, or any child, based on the sins of his father."

"I believe you," she whispered.

Her gold eyes had gone wide, and she nodded, pressing her cheek against his chest, and marking him with her scent in that way felines had about them. Javier had never felt so damn good about three little words.

I believe you. They weren't *I love you*, but it was a start. Maybe he should be the one who broke that particular ice.

"I love you, Pamela," he blurted, and the cashier stopped ringing up their purchases while he looked from Pamela's stunned face to Javier's serious one.

"Javi—"

"Not yet," he said, shaking his head as he took her hand and kissed her fingertips. "Don't say anything yet. Just know that I love you."

"Uh, will that be cash or credit?" asked the young employee, who was wearing a silly grin on his face and while Pamela giggled and hugged Javier around his waist.

"Credit, and please pay for the next customer's purchase as well," he whispered, but Pamela heard him and the squeeze she gave him made his little tradition of paying it forward during the holiday season that much sweeter.

"Thank you, sir! Merry Christmas!"

Chapter Fourteen

It took over an hour to wrap all the gifts and hide them in her small apartment, but they worked together and got it done. Afterwards, they'd ordered a couple of pizzas and cold orange soda. Her favorite.

"Would you like another slice?" Javier offered her the last of the meat lovers' pie from *Grimaldi's Pizza*, but she shook her head.

"No, I can't eat another bite," she said and watched him finish the oversized slice in four bites.

"I am always hungry. Can't help it, I am a Bear that way."

He shrugged and wiped his mouth neatly with a paper towel. She'd been embarrassed by her home, but Javi had put her worries at ease immediately. He really did not care about pomp and circumstance and seemed to genuinely like being with her.

"I mean, you're big, don't get me wrong, but there isn't an ounce of fat on you anywhere," she replied, and eyed him from head to toe.

"Fast metabolism, you know how it is," he said.

"Hardly," she looked down at her body and stopped when he growled.

"My mate's body is fucking gorgeous and no one, *not even her*, should say otherwise in front of me. This body is mine."

Javi stalked over to her on all fours from their makeshift picnic in the living room, aka her bedroom. He caged her beneath him, forcing her to lean back as he nuzzled her neck and reached out a hand, petting her from her shoulders to her breasts, belly, hips, and ass. He handled every soft curve and roll gently and expertly.

"Every inch of you is sublime," he said, and punctuated the statement with a thorough kiss that left her panting.

He sat back, eyes glittering before he rose to clean up their dinner. It took a moment for her to snap out of the trance he'd put her in, and from that cocky grin on his face, the bastard knew exactly what he was doing.

Dangerous, sexy, stunning Bear.

Mate, chuffed the Tiger.

Javier had been calling her that all day, and so far, she had yet to return the moniker. Pamela was cautious that word. She did like him, though. She was very fond of his impeccable manners and sense of style. She adored the way he was always touching her and complimenting her without it being forced or fake. Javier was not like any of the men she had ever known.

Perhaps that was one of the reasons she found it so difficult to say no to him. But it was more than that, she realized as he efficiently cleaned the remnants of their dinner and gift wrapping. He tied the garbage bag closed and replaced it before leaving her apartment to toss the full one down the chute. Before he went, he kissed her again and this time she gave into it immediately.

Hell, she damn near swooned at his every touch. He was always kissing her. He was attracted to her, which was good, but he also talked to her. That was new and exciting. They'd chatted in the car and through their meal. Being with him was easy. Fun.

He seemed to enjoy holding her hand when they shopped. And when he couldn't do that, he placed a palm on the small of her back. It was old fashioned and sweet, and it made her feel protected—taken care of, wanted even.

That was something Pamela didn't think she'd ever felt before. Then there was the sexual attraction she felt for him.

Holy flaming fart balls, did she want that man like crazy! And it was only going to get worse. She knew that from hearing the Pride's females talk. Images of their earlier love-making—that frenzied, wild passionate ride inside the restroom of her place of employment—kept flashing through her mind and damn, it had been beyond exciting. He was so damned hot. She shivered in anticipation whenever he was near her.

"What are you thinking about?" he asked in a rumbly voice that meant he knew exactly where her mind had gone.

"Mmm, I can't help it," she admitted. "But there's no time, I have to get Paulie."

"Nothing to worry about, love. We have all the time in the world. I am not going anywhere," he said and gave her another quick kiss before they left to get Paulie.

"Hello!" Pamela called inside the Pride House as she and Javier entered through the front door.

"Mommy!" Paulie came running towards them

like a little whirlwind of energy, nearly toppling her over.

"Hello, little cub. Oh, I think you've grown another inch," she teased and hugged him tight.

"I did, Mommy. I did! I ate all my chicken dinner, and Aunt Lissa says I'm gonna be a huge Tiger someday. Who's that man?"

"Hello, Paulie." Javier knelt down and extended a hand. "My name is Javier Auberon, but you can call me Javi. I am a friend of your mother."

"Hey, I got a loose tooth, wanna see?"

"I would love to," he said, and settled on the floor to get a good look.

"I ate nine chicken strips for dinner and that was more than my friends. How many can you eat?"

"Oh, I don't know. Probably thirty, but I have to keep the Bear inside of me happy."

"You have a Bear? Cool! I have a Tiger," Paulie said excitedly. "So, you like my mom?"

"I do, Paulie, very much. I like you too."

"I like you too. But you have to be nice to Mommy, and never make her cry or someday my huge Tiger will eat you up," Paulie said very seriously.

"I see. Well, I can promise you that if I ever make her cry, it will not be on purpose. I only want her to be happy. And you too, Paulie. But if I mess up, maybe you can talk to me before you eat me?" he asked, and Paulie considered his words before nodding.

Pamela bit back tears as she watched the two most important males in her life get to know each other. Paulie took Javi's hand and was now tugging him into the living room to show him the Pride House's Christmas tree.

"Hello, I'm Hunter Maverick." The Pride Neta stood in the living room with both his daughters when Javier and Paulie walked in with Pamela behind them.

"Hi Hunter! This is Javi. Oh, Mommy, Melly was pullin' my hair again," her son complained. Pamela murmured sympathetically, noting the way his eyes went to the baby, and he was smiling, so it could not have been all that bad.

"Yes, she is fond of hair-pulling," Hunter said apologetically.

"Nice to meet you, I am Javier Auberon," the Bear said politely, bowing his head in reverence to the leader of the Pride.

"Pamela? Have something to tell us?" Hunter asked, teal eyes glowing with his Tiger.

"Oh, um, well, Hunter, Paulie, Javier is my, well, he's, uh—"

Pam looked between the two men and down at her son, who was also gazing at her with his head cocked to the side. Then she froze.

"I am her friend. We are still figuring things out," Javi explained, and winked at Pamela.

"PAMELA!" the sound of her name being screamed from the kitchen set her into action and she excused herself from what had just become an awkward situation.

"Elissa? What is it?" she ran to the kitchen to see the Nari bent over a tray of what were supposed to be gingerbread Santa hats—only, *er*, they weren't.

"*Ohmygawd*," snorted Jessica, who snagged one of the cookies hot off the tray. "You made gingerbread boobs!"

"Shut up, heifer," growled Elissa, as she tried to push the cookies back into shape.

"*Dey twaste gwood though*," mumbled Jess with a mouthful of the spicy holiday treat.

"What? Don't talk with your mouthful. Is he here?" Elissa asked, addressing that last bit to Pamela.

"Who?"

"Who, she says! You know, Marion was on the

phone with Gretchen the second he left the salon. I swear that half-Troll knows everything before I do! Gretchen called Jess, who came here to tell me about your new bae—and for some reason she is still here eating me out of house and home! But Pam, I can't believe you didn't let me know you got a little *sumpin' sumpin'* last night!"

"Holy shit, Elissa, how do you talk so fast?" Pamela stared in wonder.

"It's a Hoboken thing," she mumbled, taking a bite of her own gingerbread boob. "And don't change the subject."

"Yeah, we wanna know if you got that itch of yours scratched," Jess said, snorting as she decorated another cookie with pink frosting and a cherry in the middle where the nipple went.

Pamela snorted and laughed. Jess waggled her eyebrows up and down in what was actually very disturbing before popping the frosted boob cookie into her mouth.

"So good," the redhead moaned.

"Shhh," Pamela closed the door to the kitchen and sat down. "He's a Shifter. He will hear you guys!"

"We heard he's got an accent," Elissa continued. "Is it *hawt?* Like British or like Aussie *hawt?* Come on, spill!!"

"OMG! Okay, if I tell you will you both shut up?"

"YES!! Um, yessss," they both shouted, then whispered in unison.

"*Gods, help us*," Pamela rolled her eyes, "He is from South America, Ecuador, actually. And he only has a slight accent, but it gets more pronounced when we, *um*, that is when he is *emotional*."

"OMG! Really?"

"He comes with an accent! Get it?" Elissa asked, erupting in gales of giggles at her own sense of humor.

"I will not share if you keep interrupting," Pam threatened.

"Shush, Liss. Go on, Pam. Tell us more," Jess begged.

"Okay, one thing. So, when he says my name sometimes, it's like, *holy fucking shit hawt*," Pamela said, mimicking Elissa's own Hudson County accent when she said the word hot.

"I knew it. So, his accent increases when he's fucking, right? That is so *hawt*! And he calls you Pamela, right? But like this, *Pa-mela*! Slower on the first syllable, right?"

"Elissa, no. Please shut up," she begged respectfully, but of course the Nari was on a roll.

Loveable little nut job that she was, Elissa

continued to butcher accents everywhere by repeating Pamela's name fifty-odd times. There was nothing else to be done, she supposed, so Pam just sat and stuffed a gingerbread boob into her mouth. She shook her head and repeatedly begged the Nari to please stop every few minutes. After so much abuse, Elissa screamed and the whole damn house stood still.

"AGHHHHH! I am so happy for youuuuuuuu, PA-MELA!" Elissa shouted and fanned her face.

Just then, the kitchen door opened to admit a red-faced Hunter. Javier followed, looking around anxiously. Then he tried, and failed, not to laugh. Pamela, on the other hand, wished she could disappear through the floor.

"What the hell is going on?"

"Um, nothing honey, I was just saying accents were sexy. Want a boob?" The Nari held up a cookie as a peace offering, but her mate looked pissed as hell.

"Ladies," growled Hunter, as he stalked his wife, who was trying not to giggle. "This is Javier. Jess, watch my kids while I have a word with my wife."

Hunter bent down and scooped Elissa off her chair, tossing the blonde over his shoulder before heading towards their suite of rooms on the other side of the Pride House.

"Aren't they romantic?" Jess sighed and stood up to go to the twins.

"Do you need help with them?" Pamela offered.

"Nah, Brayden's already on his way back with my order from Bear Claw Bakery. Should be here in five minutes. You guys go on, get outta here!"

"Yes, let's go, *Pa-mela*," Javier said her name in that deep husky way that made her panties go damp almost immediately with need.

Flaming fart balls!

Javier had definitely heard her talking about him to her friends.

Whoopsie.

Chapter Fifteen

The next day, Javier picked Pamela and Paulie up and drove them to New York City to see the Rockefeller Center tree and to go ice skating.

It was a spectacular day for it! The sun was shining, and the streets looked like they were etched in frosting. Lights, sparkles, giant Christmas decorations New York was famous for decked out every street and corner. Javier handled himself expertly in the bustling city and always had a protective hand on Pamela's back and on Paulie's shoulder. She shouldn't be so moved by it, but she was.

The she-Tiger inside of her loved the open display of affection and, yes, possession, too. Her beast wanted to belong to him. Hell, she already did, but Pamela was a modern woman and wasn't sure she should like that sort of thing.

Who are you kidding?

Her inner Tiger chuffed, and she rolled her eyes at the animal. Afterwards, they'd gone out to lunch and Pamela had never seen so many beautifully prepared courses as they lunched at a tiny little Chinese place that had authentic dim sum and specialty dishes. The soup dumplings were her favorite, and Paulie ate an entire duck. Then, finally, Javi brought them to FAO Schwarz to pick out a special toy.

"I can't believe he chose gifts for the twins instead of something for himself," Javier whispered to Pamela.

"I know! He is so sweet. And don't think I didn't see you buy that handheld game system for him when we supposedly weren't looking."

"Shh," Javi mock scolded.

Paulie slept soundly, clutching the carved llama Javier gave to him while sitting in the booster seat that was snug in the middle of the back row of his Mercedes truck. He'd gone out and purchased the safest model before picking them up.

Already his Bear had claimed the cub as his own, it was just a matter of formalizing everything, but his feelings were clear. His safety and happiness were tantamount to everything save Pamela's in Javier's eyes.

He loved them both with all his heart and wanted them to be a family. More than anything, he wanted her to acknowledge his claim, and maybe—if he was a very good Bear—she would claim him in turn.

"He had a great day," she whispered and smiled at the sweet cub, then looked up at Javi with flashing gold eyes that were so beautiful, they brought him to his knees.

Mate.

"Thank you for coming with me today. It means a lot," Javi told her and squeezed her hand before replacing his on the steering wheel.

"I should be thanking you. This was wonderful. You know, I have never been to the city at Christmastime," she confessed.

"What? You live so close," Javi replied, truly shocked.

"I know, but I just never had anyone special to share it with. I am glad I got to experience it with you," she said, and his chest swelled with pride.

"Do you have dinner plans?"

"Um, no," she shrugged. "Paulie was going to

make some decorations at the Pride House with some of the other kids."

"I see, do you think Elissa would mind watching him so I could take his mama out for the evening?"

"I can text her," she bit her lip and started shooting off a text to the Nari, hoping beyond hope that she would agree to watch Paulie.

She bit her lip and frowned for a moment as old worries and fears tried to wriggle their way into her mind, but Pamela was not going to allow that to happen. This was her time now. She had a past, but it was behind her. Javier and Paulie were her future. If she could just find the courage to believe in herself and in him.

Caring for her son was as natural as breathing, and what better way to show him she cared than by giving the one man in the world destined for her, the opportunity to make them a family? Could she put her heart out there and risk it all? The answer was easy as pie.

Yes, she thought to herself. Yes, she could.

Javier proved he was good with children and tonight she was going to let him show her just how *nice* having a mate could be. With any luck, that would include some very naughty times, followed by a long discussion about their future.

Pamela could not wait. Her she-Cat chuffed and yowled impatiently. Her animal wanted to mark him with her bite, to claim him as she wanted to since that first night in his arms.

Soon, she promised.

Mine, growled her inner she-Tiger.

Nerves filled her, but she calmed herself, thinking over the last few days with Javier. They were better than any Pamela had ever experienced in her life. Maybe it had to do with it being the Christmas season or maybe the Fates were finally smiling down at her.

All she knew was that every moment she spent in his company, Pamela fell more and more for the big guy. Fine, She could admit it—even if only to herself. Pamela was falling in love with him.

Javier Auberon, independent business owner and Andean Bear Shifter from Ecuador, was a wonderful man, a thoughtful lover, and apparently, he was her fated mate.

Double forking fart balls...

The truth was, he was way out of her league, or so she'd thought at first. But that was how the old Pamela thought. This Pamela was worthy of love and respect and Javier managed to deliver both while assuaging any fears she had on that front.

He was exceedingly down to earth and approachable. Had no problem flailing around the ice skating rink just to make her son laugh—she'd seen how good he was on skates and knew it was all just a front, but it was positively adorable. He had effortlessly carried her cub on his shoulders throughout their travels when Paulie had started to wilt. He'd opened every door and found a million excuses to touch her hand or back, and to steal kisses from her lips.

Javier had won Paulie over instantly with his first fumble onto the surprisingly small ice skating rink beneath the behemoth tree. After her little boy had whispered to his mother that he was afraid to fall. Her protective instincts had made her want to leave the rink, but Javier had managed to take away his fear by falling down and getting back up.

He showed her son patiently the proper way to stand after falling down, and even better, he readily accepted her son's mitted hand after Paulie wisely suggested Javier hold onto him until they *both* got the hang of it. After a few minutes, they were both skating circles around the other people who'd braved the wintry weather to experience Christmas in New York.

Pamela did alright by herself, but she loved it

when Javier had surprised her by twirling her round and round on the rink. When Paulie giggled and clapped, Javier picked him up and tossed him in the air, making her sweet boy squeal with laughter.

Oh yes, she thought with a sigh. It had been a truly magical day.

Javier was sweeter and more patient than any of the men she'd ever had in her life before. Everything he did was carried out with manners and courtesy, affection, and respect. Loving him was easy, she realized suddenly.

Sure, Pamela might've doubted her ability to make a man like Javier happy at first sight, but every time he touched her and tossed a smile her way, it was like the sun coming out in her own personal universe. Javier seemed to project his own feelings about her to the entire world freely, plainly, and she longed to do the same.

Wouldn't it be wonderful if everyone just admitted how they felt and loved each other honestly? How could she *not* love him back?

He'd already given her his bite and her she-Cat was desperate to return it. The beast scratched at her skin, wanting to sink her fangs into his skin and mark him as her own. Her heat cycle was still active and the more time she spent with him, she knew it was going to happen sooner or later. The need to claim him would hit her hard and fast.

"Good news," she turned to him and smiled. "Elissa said no problem."

"Is that all she said?" he asked with one perfect, dark brow arched.

"Not hardly," Pamela snorted. "She typed 'no problem, *Pa-mela*' and I swear, I am going to kill her," Pam groaned, unable to keep even the smallest secret from him.

He laughed easily, and she joined him, squeezing his thigh with her hand. She really loved touching him. It was new and exciting, this feeling of wanting to share everything.

If Javier was truly her fated mate, he would always want her, and she him. At least, that was what she'd learned watching the couples within the Pride. Her new friends and their mates, like the Neta and his Nari, were always so in love.

Was it wrong for Pamela to want that for herself? Was it even possible? Watching him as he laughed softly at Elissa's texted remark, Pamela felt hopeful for the first time in forever.

"I like your Nari," he said. "She is quite funny."

"You do?"

"Yes." Javi furrowed his thick brown eyebrows

thoughtfully, and once more she was struck by how handsome he was. "I like all of them. The Maverick Pride is full of feisty women and honest men. I look forward to being part of that group, Pamela. That is, the minute you say yes, of course. Then our real mating can begin, but I won't rush you, *querida*. We go at your pace, always," he murmured and kissed her palm, keen eyes on the road.

Pamela was deep in thought for most of the drive back to Maverick Point. She was once again happily surprised that Javier did not seem to mind her contemplative mood in the least. It was the first time the male she was with did not demand all her attention—*and wasn't that nice for a change?*

It was a hard fact that Javier was the only man she had ever known who had her comfort and safety at the foremost of his mind. Everything he did told her he cared, and her discussion with Elissa had confirmed it.

"You know, for a woman who was born a Shifter, you know very little about fated mates," the Nari had remarked with a hint of sadness in her voice.

"I am so sorry I didn't know you before, Pamela, but let me put your fears to rest. If your she-Tiger recognizes Javier as your mate, and his Bear does the same for you, then you are fated mates. It is practically his only biolog-

ical imperative to keep you happy, safe, and, if you're lucky, to fuck you stupid every single night." Elissa had grinned at the last bit of her speech.

Pamela was grateful for the female in so many ways. And even more so now that she understood a little more about mates. She could trust in Javier, and in her feelings for him. The future was never certain, but if she had him in her life, it would be good, that much she was sure of.

The trip home was usually just over two hours, but with holiday traffic, it took nearly three. Paulie had slept most of the way, but they stopped and peed on the side of the road with half an hour to go. Javier was so cute, he shrugged his shoulders and peed too, when Paulie was too nervous to go. He did that just so the little guy didn't feel alone. Silly as it was, she smiled and handed them both sanitizing wipes as they got into the car, and her heart beat a little faster.

Bum bum. Bum bum. Bum bum.

Was it possible for her to love him anymore?

"Mommy! Javi can make shapes in the snow with his pee!"

"What?" Pam opened her eyes wide and met Javi's shocked face.

"Uh, well—"

The expression on his face was priceless. Poor

Javi looked horribly embarrassed. Pamela laughed, and he grinned beneath his bright cheeks. She nodded at her son as he described the event, and she strapped him safely back into his seat.

"I can only make a circle, but he got a good five-point star!" Paulie enthused.

"That's very nice, baby," she said.

"Mom!"

"Oh, I mean that's nice, *young man*," she corrected her grievous error.

"About that—" Javier rubbed the back of his neck before he continued. "My brother and I used to have contests."

"Like, literal pissing contests?"

"Um—yes?"

Pamela laughed when his cheeks turned an even darker shade of red and he revved the engine, checking the empty road carefully before taking off.

"Music, Mom, please," yelled Paulie, and Javi turned on the Christmas station.

The unlikely trio started singing carols loud as they could all the way home, and it was the happiest Pamela could remember being in a very long time.

Joy to the world.

<h1 style="text-align:center">Chapter Sixteen</h1>

Getting Paulie washed and dressed in his favorite teddy bear printed footie pajamas was easy before they drove him over to the Pride House. He loved spending time with the twins and other cubs, and he loved hanging out with his Neta and Nari.

"Hey there, pal! You ready for Christmas ornament madness?" Hunter Maverick asked. The Neta answered the door and immediately earned himself a high-five from little Paulie.

"Hi Neta! Yep. I'm back. Where's Melly and Celia?"

"They are waiting for you in the living room with some of the other cubs, and our Nari is bringing out the ornaments and paint in a few minutes. Go on now," he instructed, and Paulie hooted excitedly.

He waved goodbye to his mother and Javi without even looking back. Pamela held Javier's hand and sighed as she watched his little teddy bear covered butt round the corner.

"Thank you so much, Neta," Pamela said to the Pride leader, and he smiled and nodded at her.

"You know Paulie is welcome here anytime, but if you don't mind waiting a bit before you head to dinner, I'd like a word with Javier," he asked and inclined his head. Javier straightened his shoulders, bowing his head slightly as he nodded and followed behind her inside the Pride House.

"Is everything okay?" Pamela asked.

"It will be fine," Javier said, and kissed her on the forehead before going into Hunter's office.

Pamela bit her lip and watched after the two men worriedly. She was soon called away by Elissa and to her surprise, Uncle Uzzi, who was also in the kitchen.

"Uncle Uzzi, thank you for your gingerbread cookie recipe. You know I am something of a cook, but I hate following recipes exactly, and I am afraid with baking you have to," Elissa said, and Pamela looked at the new perfect little boy and girl shaped cookies.

Not a boob in sight. Snort.

"Yes, baking is more science than cooking which is probably why I like it," laughed the wickedly ingenious Witch.

"*Pa-mela*, so glad you could make it," Elissa said and waggled her eyebrows. Pamela groaned in response.

"What is wrong with her?" Uncle Uzzi asked Pamela.

"Please excuse Elissa, Uncle Uzzi. She thinks she's got Javier's accent down," Pamela explained and rolled her eyes while Uncle Uzzi barked out a short laugh.

"No, dear, it will take more work than that to mimic his sexy South American vibrato," Uncle Uzzi told the Nari. "Well, I see you look healthy and happy, Pamela. Tell me, how are things with little *osito* going?"

"There is nothing little about that man," Elissa chimed in, and Pamela growled.

"Ooops," Pam muttered and apologized to the Nari. She covered her mouth to get her jealous kitty under control. "Sorry about that. So, um, things are good actually. He seems very fond of Paulie."

"And you? How does he feel about you?"

"He said he loves me," she blurted. "That is, he said it out loud at the store yesterday, but he hasn't repeated it again."

Pamela's heart squeezed, and warmth filled her. Javi loved her. She knew it in her soul. The words were nice to hear, but it was knowing how he felt that really wrecked her.

"OMG! That is so sweet," Elissa murmured.

"Have you said those words to him?" Uncle Uzzi asked.

"No, but I think I do. I mean, I do, I love him," Pam confessed and swallowed. "Uncle Uzzi, can I ask you something?"

"Sure, anything," the older Witch replied, testing a gingerbread cookie with a hearty moan.

"Do you think I deserve him? Do you think after everything I've done, I deserve to be happy? I mean, what if I say yes and the Fates take him away from me," she whispered.

"Oh, Pam."

Elissa's lip trembled and she went to Pamela's side and wrapped her arms around her in a hug. Before she knew it Uncle Uzzi was doing the same and Pamela's face was wet with tears, she hadn't been aware she was crying.

"Now, you listen to me, my dear. That is not how this works. The Fates match up pairs, but we choose our mates. Now, that said, I'm Javi's honorary uncle, and since he is your fated mate, that makes me your uncle too. You are more than deserving of every bit of happiness, light, and joy you can get out of this life, you hear?"

"Yes, I hear," she replied, laughing through her tears.

"Good, now where is he?"

"I don't know. Hunter took him into his office," Pamela said.

Suddenly, a loud sound like a huge crash followed by shouting and growls had the three of them rushing out of the kitchen. Pamela did not hesitate, she pushed the door open to the Neta's office and gasped at the sight before her.

Javier was on the floor beneath an angry male. Then he was on top of the man—Lance, she identified—and he was smashing his fist repeatedly into the young Tiger's face. Pierce was in the melee too, having Javi's neck in a chokehold, which Brayden was trying to loosen. Hunter had just opened his mouth but turned to jump in front of the women and Uncle Uzzi, taking a protective stance.

"We better get them outside," Uncle Uzzi said, watching the fight with more than average concern.

"We need to get them to stop!" Pamela countered.

"Too late for that," the Witch shook his head and pointed to Brayden. "Open the sliding door quick. If we don't get Javi outside, he's going to break through the wall—"

"What the heck are you talking about, Uncle Uzzi?" Pamela asked wide-eyed while her mate snarled angrily as his features sharpened and his body began to grow.

Pierce had already changed into his Tiger and Lance was trying, but Javi had a too-tight grip on the younger man's throat. His chest was heaving, and he was growling really fucking loudly.

"Someone tell me what the fuck is going on!" Hunter roared as he did his best to shield his mate, Pamela, and Uzzi.

Brayden had the sliding door open, and he went outside to shift into his Bear, trying to get Javi's attention. Pamela moved to go to her mate, but Hunter grabbed her arm and pulled her back sharply. He was trying to protect her, she knew, but judging from the sound Javier just made that was not the smartest thing he could have done. Javier did not seem too thrilled about the Neta manhandling her.

"Uh oh," Uncle Uzzi whispered.

The resounding roar that came from Javi's ursine mouth was loud enough to shake the rafters. Pamela gasped as Pierce tackled him, catching him off guard. The Tiger managed to push him outside to meet Brayden's Black Bear, Pierce's Tiger, and now Lance's Tiger.

But by the time he stopped skidding across the snow, Pamela realized it did not matter if he was facing three or thirty shifters. Javier Auberon had been hiding something from her—and the secret was out.

Her mate was a fucking giant.

"Uncle Uzzi?"

"Remember when you asked me why I called a grown ass man *osito*? Well, truth be told, it was an ironic nickname. Javier is special, even for a Shifter." The infamous matchmaker nodded at the proof of his claim and Pamela stared in shocked wonder.

"*Osito* is not really a little Bear at all. You see, he carries a special genetic quirk, a throwback gene in his DNA. Javi is a *Dire Andean Bear Shifter*, dear. His Bear is a prehistoric version of his Clan's animal."

"*OHMYGAWD!* He's fucking huge. I knew it," Elissa shouted, and elbowed Pamela and she just nodded.

"Yes. He is big, and so beautiful, look at those facial markings," Pamela whispered.

"Uh, Pamela, I understand seeing your mate's animal is pretty special the first time around, but can you stop him from killing my Beta and guards?" Hunter asked, watching as Javi wiped the floor with three of the toughest Shifters she had ever met.

"Oh, shit, yeah, um, yes, I better get on that," she said, and went outside through the unfortunately broken sliding door that led to the yard.

"Javier?" she called, and her giant mate stopped pummeling the others and turned to face her.

The Beta of the Pride and the two guards backed off but circled the perimeter, causing her anxious mate to get all growly. Pamela rolled her eyes and waved them away.

"Guys, get out of here. He won't hurt me. Will you, big guy?" she murmured as the giant animal lumbered forward, bumping her belly with his enormous head.

She reached out and stroked his thick fur, enjoying the satisfied sound he made when she scratched his ears.

"You are so handsome, mate," she purred softly in her throat and Javier's Bear grunted happily.

"Mommy!"

"Paulie," she whispered, eyes wide, she turned to stop him, but it was too late.

Her son was racing across the yard, and the little cub had vaulted himself across the snow, jumping right on Javier's giant back. Everyone went quiet and Hunter appeared in his Tiger, the massive Cat growling quietly as everyone waited to see how the Dire Bear would react to the cub.

Pamela, however, was not surprised by his actions. She'd had no doubts about how her son would be received by Javier's beautiful, powerful, and enormous beast. The giant creature just laid down in the snow, like an overgrown puppy, and let her cub climb all over him.

Paulie giggled and squealed as he sat on top of Javi's shoulders, pulling his ears until they started to shrink. Soon the boy was sitting on the man, and Pamela smiled as Elissa came outside and tossed towels to the bunch of naked dudes.

"Put the sausages away, boys. There are little eyes around."

"Elissa," Hunter growled, squeaking when she pinched him right on the ass. Pamela giggled at the display. She wanted to be them when she grew up.

"I like your Bear," Paulie told Javi with a wide grin.

"He likes you too," Javier returned with real affection, making Pamela's heart melt.

"You gonna marry us?" her cub asked.

Pamela's cheeks burned with embarrassment at her son's innocent inquiry. Still, she bit her lip and waited for the answer. Yes, they were mates, but that didn't always translate into more.

She'd always dreamed of a real home, a husband, and a family of her own. Their eyes met and Javier's glittered at her as he cocked his head, reading her like the open book she was.

Damn.

Was he going to say something? She ignored the quiet as everyone went inside, giving the trio some much needed privacy. All the while her pulse raced, and heart pounded. This was the scariest moment of Pamela's life, and that was saying something.

Heart on the line, she waited impatiently while Javi fastened the towel tightly around his hips as fat snowflakes started to fall down on them.

"Well?" Paulie asked.

Insert impatient yowl here.

Her inner Tiger hissed and chuffed, but Pamela didn't know what to do or say, so she remained motionless. Waiting.

Mate?

Chapter Seventeen

Fifteen minutes earlier...

"So, Javier, how long will you be visiting us?" Hunter questioned him the second the office door had shut.

He turned around the room, noting he and the Neta were not alone. In fact, there were two Tiger Shifters and one Black Bear Shifter waiting in the office. If he did not know better, he would've thought this was some kind of shakedown.

Javi had done business with some dangerous people over the years, but these were not just men. These were powerful Shifters, and they made up his mate's Pride. He would do his best to remain respectful and treat them accordingly.

"I have just purchased a home in town. So, I guess

you could say I am planning to be here for quite a while."

"Is that so?" the youngest looking of the bunch growled. "I hear you think you can just come here and start filling Pamela's head up with shit about being your mate, hotshot."

Javier's inner Bear snarled and snapped inside of him. He did not care for the way the stranger spoke about Pamela. Possessive feelings rose quickly inside him, his Bear fast to anger. That was probably because their bond was not complete, and the beast was still acting on instinct.

"She is mine," Javi growled.

So much for easygoing, he thought, and faced the younger man. He stepped forward, going toe to toe with the taller, wider Javier. A foolish move for anyone—even a Tiger.

In the wild, Andean Bears were one of the smallest species. Shy, loners who preferred the solitude of the forest to living in groups. Shifters were different. Andean Bears especially. Almost four times bigger than their wild cousins, Andean or Spectacled Bear Shifters were almost half a ton when in their fur. But Javier was twice that.

He was actually very unique. Every now and again a rare mutation caused one of his kind to Shift into a prehistoric version of his animal, a Dire Bear to be exact. Right then, his inner beast was growling in fury.

This little pussy had dared insult his mate. The man had the gall to utter her name in Javier's presence. Fuck no. His Bear did not like it one little bit.

Rrrrroooaaaaarrr!

Typically, he tried to control his urge for violence, but Javier was seriously pissed off. One more snicker from the punk and he would not be responsible for his actions.

"She's been used and abused too much already. No fucking playboy is going to waltz into town and mess with one of our own," the Tiger Shifter snarled. "You best fuck off, teddy bear. That little she-Cat is not for you."

That was it. The leash Javier had around his beast snapped. He vaulted over the floor and had the man by the throat. Of course, that meant another one of the Neta's guards attempted to subdue him.

Not that two alone could do that. He didn't want to cause any more damage than necessary, but this little shit needed to be taught a lesson, and Javier was just the man to do it.

The sounds of footsteps running towards the office, where he was currently wrestling two of the

Tiger Shifters, barely registered. He heard Elissa, the Nari of the Pride, gasp, and Hunter growled angrily, barking orders, but Javi was not under his rule yet.

He planned to be. Just as soon as his feisty mate claimed his furry ass, but until then, he disregarded the order to cease the fighting. Uncle Uzzi shouted something, and he felt a small zap of the male Witch's powers, but the beast was too angry.

Whatever.

He didn't really have time to think. The Bear wouldn't listen, anyway. The animal wanted recompense for the Tiger's mouthy words. He needed them to understand that regardless of the past, Pamela was his now and forevermore. No one talked about her. Ever.

The females were still yelling when he turned and saw Hunter grab Pamela's arm. Whatever bit of control he'd had fled in that moment. Javier roared, but since he had allowed himself to get distracted, one of the Cats tackled his big furry Bear right outside. Now he was separated from his Pamela with three Shifters on his ass. And that really pissed off his Bear.

Fuck it.

He embraced his Dire Bear's power and roared his fury. Swatting the little fucker's tail and pinning him under his bulk. The Black Bear would cause some issue, but the Cats, fast and lethal as they were, were simply no match for his strength and size. Then the strangest thing happened. His mate yelled, and he turned to see her cub—*his cub, the Bear corrected*—running over to him.

That stopped his animal like nothing else could. The sweet-smelling little boy climbed up Javier's bulky, fur-covered body with enthusiasm. His little sneakers dug into parts that Javi would rather not admit, and yes, he yanked his ears and stuck a finger up one of his nostrils, but the Bear was overjoyed. The huge beast chuffed happily. His animal more than willing and ready to be a playground for their cub.

Eventually, Javi changed back into his skin, breathing heavily, and meeting his mate's awestruck stare as he gently placed the boy on the ground. He knew he had explaining to do, but nothing could've prepared him for what came out of Paulie's mouth next.

"You gonna marry us?"

Marriage? It had never occurred to him that traditional marriage was something he would ever want, but as soon as his cub uttered the words, he knew there was only one possible answer.

"Well?"

Paulie interrupted his thoughts and he realized he had yet to respond. Javier made sure the towel was tight around his hips before kneeling down to look Paulie in the eye, ignoring the big ears of the adults who, though they'd left, were still close enough to listen in.

Warmth filled him as he realized the remarks the young Tiger had made were to test him. This was Pamela's home, her Pride, and they cared and protected her. Yes, he saw that now, and he respected them all the more for it.

"Marriage is a big step, Paulie, but we are Shifters, you understand this, yes?" He waited for the cub to nod before he continued.

"We do things a little differently. You see, your mother is my fated mate. That means she is a part of my very soul, like my Bear. I love her more than anything, and since you are a part of her, that means I love you, too."

"You do?"

"Yes, sweet cub, I do. I would very much like to marry your mother, but I think I need your permission first. Would that be okay with you, Paulie, if your mama and I get mated and married?"

"Does that mean you would be my dad?" Paulie

looked down at his hands, but Javier lifted his chin and met his golden stare that was so much like his mother's it made his heart squeeze inside his chest.

"I would very much like to be your dad," he said and blinked back tears.

"Okay, but if you make her sad, you will be in trouble," promised the little boy.

"Paulie," Pamela ruffled her son's hair, and the boy looked up, giving her a wide smile.

Javier reached out and took her hand in his, keeping his place on the floor, he inhaled her cinnamon honey scent and spilled his guts right then and there.

"Pamela Brown, I have known since the first time I saw you that you were my fated mate. I love you, I have loved you since that very first time, and I promise I always will. Your safety and happiness, yours, Paulie's, and whatever other children we have, will always be my first priority. I need you, *querida*. I love you. Will you marry me?"

Pamela covered her mouth on a sob, and he waited patiently while she nodded her head and wiped at the tears that streamed down her face. Javi grinned and stood up, cupping her face in his hands and bent his head. Then, suddenly, pain exploded in his right shin.

"Ouch!"

"Paulie!"

"You made Mommy cry! It's my job to protect her," the indignant boy said and looked at both adults with a confused expression.

"Oh, sweetie, no, I am not crying because Javier did anything wrong," Pamela explained, and bent down and hugged her son. "In fact, I am crying because he made me very, very happy."

"Oh! Like when I draw pictures for you, and you hang them on the fridge and get all wishy washy?" he said, then grinned mischievously and shrugged at Javier.

"Sorry, Dad!" he giggled and ran away, and Javier stood there shocked.

"He called me 'Dad'," he whispered.

"Is that okay? I can talk to him if you'd rather—"

"It is more than okay," he said and wrapped her in his arms. "Come on, let's go on our date."

"Okay, I'd like that," Pamela smiled up at him and he kissed her soundly on the mouth.

"Everyone happy now?" Uncle Uzzi came outside with a bundle in his hands and the newly engaged couple smiled widely at him.

"Yes, we're going to go to dinner now," Javi told him.

"Wonderful," Uncle Uzzi said, watching amusedly as they walked away. "*Osito*, don't you think you should put on some clothes first?"

"Oh crap! Yes, uh, I will be right back," Javi said, blushing and turning to accept the package Uzzi held with a sheepish grin. "Thank you, please excuse me for a moment," he said and ran inside to dress.

"Well, dear?"

"Uncle Uzzi, you were right, as usual," Pamela replied happily.

"This Christmas is definitely going to be the best one I ever had!"

Epilogue

"I still can't believe you bought the house," Pamela sighed, and stretched.

Javier's cock stood at attention at the subtle move of her curvaceous body. Fuck, he was one lucky Bear. The little she-Cat was gorgeous inside and out. He turned on his side and rested his hand on her hip before leaning in to capture her kiss-swollen lips.

They never made it to the restaurant, but that was okay, because Javier had his staff stock the fridge earlier that day. Tomorrow was Christmas Eve, and he'd intended on handing his mate the keys to their beautiful new home then, but he couldn't wait.

"You are satisfied, then?" he asked.

"Oh, I am satisfied, and I plan to be satisfied again." *Kiss.*

"And again."

Kiss kiss.

"And again."

Kiss kiss kiss.

Pamela growled and giggled as she licked the seam of his lips until he opened them. Javier groaned against her tongue.

His sexy little mate did the most wonderful things to him whenever they kissed or touched. It was like he was perfectly attuned to her body and soul, and vice versa. The kiss grew hotter as she pressed her hardened nipples against his hair-roughened chest and Javi growled louder. Need and desire swelled, as did his ever growing love for her.

"Need you, mate," she moaned and brushed her lips across the new mating mark she'd just given him.

His Bear grunted happily, satisfied now that she'd claimed him. Her touch sent shivers down his spine and his cock grew harder still. The scent of her arousal increased as she mounted him and slid her slick pussy lips along his thick length.

"Fuck, *kitten,* you'll finish me before I get inside

you," he growled and nipped her lower lip, but his naughty little mate didn't stop.

Instead, she increased her pace. Her hot, wet sex glided across his shaft from root to tip.

Slide, grind, swirl, in a steadily building rhythm until his fingernails pricked her hips and lifted her slightly. Her amber eyes glowed gold with her she-Tiger and then she slammed down, encompassing him in her heat.

Javier bucked his hips, driving deep, filling his sexy mate until she was purring his name and the sound of skin slapping against skin and their hearts pounding in time filled his ears. Her pussy quivered, squeezing him as her orgasm claimed her.

"Mine," he roared, chasing her to completion.

Javier filled her with his seed, hoping against hope that tonight it would take root, and together, they would begin to grow their family.

"I love you, Javi," she whispered against his skin as she slumped against him, too tired to move.

"I love you so much, *Pa-mela*," he said, enunciating his Latin accent in a way that had her giggling happily against him.

"Merry Christmas, my mate."

Pamela looked up at him with her amber eyes shining and he knew it would be a Merry Christmas indeed, for Pamela, for Paulie, and for Javier, from now until eternity.

*B*ack in his mansion, where his staff was taking down the decorations from the ball...

Uncle Uzzi sat sipping the special vintage wine his nephew had brought him from Quito. He scrolled through the photos *osito* had sent him after Javier, Pamela, and Paulie had received the Christmas present he'd sent.

A Labrador was definitely going to complete the little family until Pamela was ready to announce her secret news. Uncle Uzzi grinned as he imagined the set of twins the she-Cat would deliver, one Tiger and one spectacled Andean Bear—*perhaps with a certain genetic mutation.*

Only time would tell that. Uzzi sighed happy for them both. Multiples were common for feline Shifters, especially when conception occurred during the female's heat.

His mind wandered as he opened the next email and read the thank you note Gabriel Auberon, the Baron, had sent him in return for him accepting his invitation to vacation with him for the new year.

Yes, Uncle Uzzi thought, *this was going to be a very special case.*

Cards from all the couples he helped match up were hanging above the hearth and the softly glowing fire there. Uncle Uzzi hummed Christmas carols and sat under the brightly lit Christmas tree while he made his travel plans.

It had been a very good year, and he could not wait to see what came next.

"To the future, liebling." Uzzi lifted his glass and toasted his dear wife, who he knew was smiling down at him.

As long as he could bring joy and love to others, the future would always be bright.

T*he end.* \

Did you enjoy this story? Check out the rest of the Maverick Pride Tales today! And keep on the lookout for more titles in this steamy PNR series.

& You can expect the new edition of Shake That Sass and a brand new take on The Wyvern Protection Unit real soon!

Beware... Here Be Dragons!

The Falk Clan Tales began as my stories surrounding four dragon Brothers and how they find their one true mates, but when a long lost brother arrives on the scene, followed by a few more Shifters…what can I say? The more the merrier!

Each Dragon's chest is marked with his rose, the magical link to his heart and his magic. They each have a matching gemstone to go with it.

She's given up on love, but he's just begun.

In *The Dragon's Valentine* we meet the eldest Falk brother, Callius. He is on a mission to find a Castle and his one true mate, one he can trust with his diamond rose....

His heart is frozen; can she change his mind about love?

In *The Dragon's Christmas Gift* our attention shifts to Alexsander, the youngest brother of the four. He has resigned himself to a life alone, until he meets *her*.

Some wounds run deep, can a Dragon's heart be unbroken?

The Dragon's Heart is the story of Edric Falk who has vowed never to love again, but that changes when he meets his feisty mate, Joselyn Curacao.

She just wants a little fun, he's looking for a lifetime.

We finally meet Nikolai Falk and his sexy Shifter mate in *The Dragon's Secret*.

Now available in a boxed set.

Guess what…. I've got more Dragons on the way!

Look for The Dragon's Treasure now available, and the upcoming The Dragon's Dream and The Dragon's Surprise!

Wolf Bride: The Story of Ailis and Eoghan A Macconwood Pack Tale 1

Summer Bite: A Macconwood Pack Tale 2

His Winter Mate: A Macconwood Pack Tale 3

Snow Angel: A Macconwood Pack Tale 4

Charley's Baby Surprise: A Macconwood Pack Tale 5

Home for the Howlidays: A Macconwood Pack Tale 6

A Silver Wedding: A Macconwood Pack Tale 7

Mine Furever: A Macconwood Pack Tale 8

A Furry Little Christmas: A Macconwood Pack Tale 9

Also available in two boxed sets:

The Macconwood Pack Tales Volume 1

Shifters Furever: The Macconwood Pack Tales Volume 2

The Falk Clan Tales:

The Dragon's Valentine: A Falk Clan Novel 1

The Dragon's Christmas Gift: A Falk Clan Novel 2

The Dragon's Heart: A Falk Clan Novel 3

The Dragon's Secret: A Falk Clan Novel 4

The Dragon's Treasure: A Falk Clan Novel 5

Dragon Mates: The Falk Clan Series Boxed Set Books 1-4

The Bear Claw Tales:

Bearly Breathing: A Bear Claw Tale 1

Bearly There: A Bear Claw Tale 2

Bearly Tamed: A Bear Claw Tale 3

Bearly Mated: A Bear Claw Tale 4

Also available in a boxed set:

The Complete Bear Claw Tales (Books 1-4)

The Barvale Clan Tales:

Polar Opposites: The Barvale Clan Tales 1

Polar Outbreak: The Barvale Clan Tales 2

Polar Compound: A Barvale Clan Tale 3

Polar Curve: A Barvale Clan Tale 4

Also available in a boxed set:

The Barvale Clan Tales (Books 1-4)

Barvale Holiday Tales:

A Bear For Christmas

Hers To Bear

Thank You Beary Much

Also available in a boxed set:

The Barvale Holiday Tales (Books 1-3)

Purely Paranormal Romance Books:

Marked by the Devil: Purely Paranormal Romance Books

Mated to the Dragon King: Purely Paranormal Romance
Books

Claimed by the Demon: Purely Paranormal Romance Books

Christmas with a Devil, a Dragon King, & a Demon: Purely Paranormal Romance Books

Vampire Lover: Purely Paranormal Romance Books

Grizzly Lover: Purely Paranormal Romance Books

Hot Dire Wolf Nights: Purely Paranormal Romance Books

Christmas With Her Chupacabra: Purely Paranormal Romance Books

The Wardens of Terra:

Bound by Air: The Wardens of Terra Book 1

Star Kissed: A Wardens of Terra Short

Waterlocked: The Wardens of Terra Book 2

Moon Kissed: A Wardens of Terra Short

*Now in a boxed set and in audio!

The Maverick Pride Tales:

Purrfectly Mated

Purrfectly Kissed

Purrfectly Trapped

Purrfectly Caught

Dire Wolf Mates:

Shake That Sass

Breaking Sass

Pinch of Sass

Kickin' Sass

<u>Wyvern Protection Unit:</u>

Gift Wrapped Protector: WPU 1

<u>Standalones:</u>

The Enforcer

Blood Song: A Sanguinem Council Book

Spring Fling (co-written with P. Mattern)

<u>EveL Worlds:</u>

Chinchilla and the Devil: A FUCN'A Book

Sammi and the Jersey Bull: A FUCN'A Book

Mouse and the Ball: A FUCN'A Book

<u>The Guardians of Chaos:</u>

Wolf Shield: Guardians of Chaos Book 1

Dragon Shield: Guardians of Chaos Book 2

Stallion Shield: Guardians of Chaos Book 3

Panther Shield: Guardians of Chaos 4

Witch Shield: Guardians of Chaos 5

<u>Howl's Romance</u>

Mated to the Werewolf Next Door: A Howl's Romance

The Tiger King's Christmas Bride

Claiming His Virgin Mate: Howls Romance

<u>Shifters Unleashed Boxed Sets</u>

Check out these amazing anthologies where you can find some of my books and the works of other awesome authors!

Midnight Magic Anthology (Water Witch)

Rituals & Runes Anthology (Air Witch)

<u>Island Stripe Pride</u>

Tiger Claimed

Tiger Denied

<u>NYC Shifter Tales</u>

Cuff Linked

Sealed Fate

<u>A Howlin' Good Fairytale Retelling</u>

Sweet As Candy (as seen in Once Upon An Ever After)

<u>Coming Soon:</u>

Asterion

For Fangs Sake

Hungry As Her Python: Magic and Mayhem Universe

The Dragon's Surprise

The Dragon's Dream

Bearing Gifts

If The Shoe Fits: A Howlin' Good Fairytale Retelling

Vampire Shield: Guardians of Chaos 6

Chickee and the Paparazzi: FUCN'A

The Wolf's Winter Wish: A Macconwood Pack Tale

The Hybrid Assassin

Tempted By Her Protector: WPU 2

Alien Protector: WPU 3

Elvish Protector: WPU 4

Thrilled By Her Protector: WPU 5

Tiger Rejected

<u>Young Adult Urban Fantasy Books:</u>

Wolf Moon: A Grazi Kelly Novel Book 1

Hunter Moon: A Grazi Kelly Novel Book 2

Rebel Moon: A Grazi Kelly Novel Book 3

Winter Moon: A Grazi Kelly Novel Book 4

Chasing The Moon: A Grazi Kelly Short 5

Blood Moon: A Grazi Kelly Novel 6

*Get all 6 books NOW AVAILABLE IN A BOXED SET:

The Complete Grazi Kelly Novel Series

Casting Magic: The Angela Tanner Files 1

Keeping Magic: The Angela Tanner Files 2

<u>G'Witches Magical Mysteries Series</u>

Co-written with P. Mattern

G'Witches

G'Witches 2: The Harpy Harbinger

G'Witches 3: Summoning Secrets

Excerpt from *Wolf Shield: Guardians of Chaos*

What a day! Fergie McAndrews headed towards the pick-up truck she'd borrowed from her roommate for work that morning.

Of course, the thirty-thousand dollar certified used luxury car she'd splurged on earlier in the year was in the shop. Again.

Just another in a long line of bad decisions. After leaving a perfectly good job for a startup company, she was laid off three weeks ago and had to borrow money from her parents to pay rent. Wasn't that humiliating?

"This is the last time, Ferg," her step-monster had said after she'd Venmo'd the money to her.

God forbid the mechanic call and tell her the car

was ready. She wouldn't be able to pick it up for another week. That was when she got her first paycheck from her newest gig at L-Corp. Not a startup, but an older company with new offices in Bayonne, which was only a half-hour commute.

But to commute, you needed a car. Fergie had no choice but to borrow the old pick-up from her best friend and roommate, Jessenia Banks. It wasn't like she needed the truck. She worked from home these days. Besides, Fergie promised to fill it up and have it washed.

She huffed out a breath. It'd been a really long day. A crappy one too. Fergie wanted to love her new job. Really, she did. But so far, it was the pits. If Fergie wanted to be a librarian, she would've been one.

Research was her jam. Well, when it was interesting. She had a knack for sniffing out information and compiling easy-to-read spreadsheets and timelines. It wasn't the hard work that annoyed her. Her complaint was the content. The actual stuff her new boss had her looking up. It was beyond boring.

Why an enormous conglomerate like L-Corp needed old land surveys, cross-referenced with newspaper reports on accidents, crimes, etcetera.

She had no idea. She'd been at it for weeks now. So far, she'd researched six locations given via GPS coordinates across Hudson County. Her new boss wanted everything, every little insignificant piece of information she could dig up.

That was the easy part. It was the hassle of the actual job that really made her want to give up. Every day she had to drive to Bayonne to pick up her work laptop she'd dropped off the night before with all of that day's findings. Every single night they wiped her computer clean.

Like she was going to run away with the secrets of what happened on 2nd and Washington sixty-years ago. Can you say paranoid? Ugh.

Fergie had always looked forward to working for a huge global company. It was supposed to be her ticket out of the Garden State. Traveling the globe, seeing new things, visiting far-off places was always a secret dream of hers. Well, that, and having her own walk-in closet full of gorgeous designer shoes.

Best secret dream evah! In her opinion, anyway. What woman didn't love shoes? Fergie hummed as she daydreamed about rows and rows of Blahnik's, Jimmy Choo's, Garavani's, Ferragamo's, and her personal favorites, Louboutin's on every shelf!

Don't judge. Fergie wasn't shallow, she just liked pretty things. Haters gonna hate. But every time she ran across a thrift or second-chance store, she'd search high and low to see what they had. That was how she'd scored the pumps on her feet.

They made her feel good about herself. Being five-foot two-inches short with more curves than a racetrack, Fergie had had more than her fair share of self-esteem issues growing up. Alright, so she was chubby. She could admit that proudly now.

If everyone looked the same, the world would be one boring as hell place. Fergie liked herself perfectly fine these days, in spite of all the times her step-monster tried to make her diet growing up. So she liked food and shoes. Big deal.

She worked hard to feed and clothe herself, so as far as she was concerned, no one had a right to comment. So what if she wanted some excitement in her life? Fergie was aware she was better off than most, but what was wrong with having goals?

She'd spent a lot of time thinking about how a woman like her could have an adventure. Travelling was the only thing she could think of. Of course, she'd been hoping this job would be the answer to that. Even travelling for work was better than being stuck.

Sigh.

So far, her plans had fallen flat, but hey, at least she was earning a paycheck. Her new boss, Mr. Offner, might be a strange man, but he signed her checks, and that was enough for now. Fergie had never seen more than a glimpse of him. All of her instructions usually came via email.

Most of the time she was able to compile her research quickly, then she'd head back to the office to organize it into neat little spreadsheets, and finally, she'd hand it all in with her laptop. But not today.

Mr. Offner sent her an email detailing everything she could dig up on one of the oldest places on record in the county. Of course, land surveys that old, along with police reports, newspaper articles, deeds, and sales records were nowhere she could easily access them.

After wasting hours at both the court house and municipal building, Fergie had been directed to the *second* public library. Apparently anything over a hundred years old was filed away in the godforsaken place. She'd been shocked to find an entire room filled with musty old archives. And wouldn't you know it, there was no cell service and no internet access. Plus, their phone lines were down. She'd had to photograph each page using her cell. When she got home later, she would send those photos like a fax to her boss along with her spreadsheet. If she could manage that before collapsing into bed.

Excerpt from Grizzly Lover

"Resa," Oliver fisted the note he'd found tucked under the secondhand keyboard he'd just finished paying off.

The instrument sat against one wall of the cramped room, right beside the only window in the small Brooklyn Heights apartment he'd been renting the past six months since he came to the city.

For a Grizzly Bear Shifter used to the wilds of the woods as his backyard, it was quite the change, but he just had to try to see if he could make a go of his music. Oliver had always been gifted with a good ear, but even as a cub, his mother had encouraged him to go and seek his destiny.

Brooklyn Heights was as close to Manhattan as he could afford with his meager savings, but what did money matter anyway? Especially when there was music to be written. The window faced the south brick wall of another small apartment complex identical to his.

It didn't matter what it looked like outside, as long as he was able to breathe some fresh air. At least on the fifth floor, it was somewhat fresher than the heavily congested streets below.

She was gone. His mind registered that fact as he took in the empty room. She'd left.

"No," he growled, and aimed his fist at the tiled counter top, cracking a few of the old ceramic squares in the process. Mrs. Goldstein, the landlady, would be pissed when she saw that.

Oliver's Bear roared inside of him and his heart contracted painfully in his chest. It was worse than being sucker punched by Thor his idiot cousin, who was as big and strong as his namesake. Why would Teresa say such cruel things? He couldn't believe it, couldn't fathom his sweet Resa saying such foul callous words about their relationship. He read the hated missive one more time.

Oliver,

It was fun while it lasted, but even you can't be so naïve as to think I could find true love with a nobody. I just wanted to get back at my father. Don't bother looking for me or calling, I will have already changed my number.

Teresa

Yes, it was her handwriting. He closed his eyes on the wave of anguish that washed over him. Gasping, he sunk to his knees while the beast inside of him roared and sTimped his massive claws in fury.

Mate, his Bear cried out, but Oliver refused to answer his other half.

How could she just leave him like this? He'd been so sure of her, of them. He was positive that she loved him too. Being with her was everything to him. She was his fated mate. It was the first time he had ever tasted happiness. A taste that was bitter now that he knew it was all one-sided.

The first time he'd seen the golden-haired beauty, Oliver's Grizzly Bear had stood up and taken notice. The second he'd breathed in her peaches and cream scent, his animal had roared one single word in his mind's eye that would change Oliver's life forever.

Mate.

Following his heart, he'd approached the soft spoken, elegantly dressed Teresa Witherspoon after spying her at the park day after day. She'd sit on one of the cleaner benches and read from a book of seventeenth century cavalier poets.

"You like Lovelace? Looking at you I pictured a Donne fan," Oliver said when he'd finally found the nerve to approach her.

"Spiritualist poetry doesn't appeal as much to me I guess. I like Lovelace and Suckling. They're fun and witty."

"But they're just trying to get in a girl's pants with their poetry. You approve?" he grinned.

"It's not so much the seduction that appeals to me, it's the living in the moment. Carpe diem and all that," she shrugged.

There was something so tragically sad about her that his heart had squeezed in his chest with longing. He'd wanted to make her smile. Heck, he even pretended to stumble in the grass, laid himself flat just to get her to walk over and touch him. And she had, put her soft, long hands right on him to see if he was alright. He'd stolen a kiss and had never looked back. Until now. The dream was over. She'd left him.

Oliver's Bear roared in his grief. That last night they were together, he'd told her the truth about what he was. The fact that there were more things in the world than she had ever imagined.

Oliver Pax had committed a most grievous sin against his Clan. He'd confessed to a normal, a human woman, that he was a Grizzly Bear Shifter.

It was allowed under certain circumstances, like when the woman in question was your fated mate. He'd thought she'd taken it well, after all, they'd made wild, passionate love immediately after. Hell, he'd been so caught up in the moment, he'd marked her with his bite, tying himself to her irrevocably, but now she was gone.

What would become of him? Would he go mad like so many other Shifters who'd lost their mates? He had heard the stories. The tales of broken matings and rogue Shifters who needed to be put down.

Oliver tipped the bottle of whiskey back emptying its fiery contents down his throat. Then he threw the hated thing across the room. Something about the muted violence of the act satisfied his animal's need for savagery. The Bear inside of him wanted to tear the whole world down, but maybe work would be a better outlet, he thought.

Oliver sat down at his banged-up keyboard and began to play. He poured out his bruised heart. Wrote lyrics and tied them together with a fairy tale as old as they come. The Beast of Brooklyn Heights was born that day. And the rest, as they say, was history.

Excerpt from Code Wolf

"Are you fuckin' with me?"

"No, Randall, I assure you I am not fuckin' with you," Rafe Maccon eased his immense frame back into his oversized, black leather chair and narrowed his ice blue eyes at his Third and one of his oldest friends. How long had he known the man sitting in front of him?

Randall had come to Maccon City when Rafe was about ten, he looked the same then as he did now. Tall at six foot three inches, muscular, and more than a little intimidating to the Wolves under him with his long beard and equally long dark brown hair.

Rafe, however, was the Alpha. He was more amused than intimidated by his surly friend.

"A vacation?! What the fuck am I gonna do on a vacation? Come on, Rafe, this is bullshit!"

The door to Rafe's private office flew open and in strolled a very happy, very pregnant Charley Maccon, Rafe's wife. The Alpha's eyes glowed as they landed on his positively glowing mate. She wore a long, flowy dress. The shade was a pale-yellow color that, Randall admitted to himself, looked damn good with her creamy complexion and curly dark hair.

Their Alpha Female was quite something. There wasn't a Wolf Guard in the place who wouldn't lay down his/her life for her.

"Well, maybe you should consider a vacation to be a relaxing experience, Randy," she dropped a kiss on Randall's cheek and walked past him, over to her husband whom she kissed full on the mouth.

The way his Alpha's eyes homed in on her when she opened the door was nothing compared to the hungry gaze that followed her across the room.

Randall had noticed it took a while for Rafe to get used to his mate's habit of greeting everyone with a kiss or hug. Wolves were protective of their mates, but Randall thought his Alpha was doing an exceedingly good job of hiding his tension. Were-wolves did not share very well.

Charley; however, had stood firm. That was the

way she was raised, and she wasn't going to change for any, how had she put it? Neanderthal brow-beating husband, regardless of how cute his ass was!

Randall had no direct knowledge if the "cute ass" statement was true or not. And he didn't want to know. He liked Charley though, had from the beginning. He was musically inclined and often took to one of the common rooms to strum his guitar or play a few keys on the piano.

About the Author

C.D. Gorri is a USA Today Bestselling author of steamy paranormal romance and urban fantasy. She is the creator of the Grazi Kelly Universe.

Join her mailing list here: https://www.cdgorri.com/newsletter

An avid reader with a profound love for books and literature, when she is not writing or taking care of her family, she can usually be found with a book or tablet in hand. C.D. lives in her home state of New Jersey where many of her characters or stories are based. Her tales are fast paced yet detailed with satisfying conclusions.

If you enjoy powerful heroines and loyal heroes who face relatable problems in supernatural settings, journey into the Grazi Kelly Universe today. You will find sassy, curvy heroines and sexy, love-driven heroes who find their HEAs between the pages. Werewolves, Bears, Dragons, Tigers, Witches, Romani, Lynxes, Foxes, Thunderbirds, Vampires, and many more Shifters and supernatural creatures dwell within her worlds. The most important thing is every mate in this universe is fated, loyal, and true lovers always get their happily ever afters.

Want to know how it all began? Enter the Grazi Kelly Universe with Wolf Moon: A Grazi Kelly Novel or pick up Charley's Christmas Wolf and dive into the Macconwood Pack Novel Series today.

For a complete list of C.D. Gorri's books visit her website here:

https://www.cdgorri.com/complete-book-list/

Thank you and happy reading!

del mare alla stella,
    C.D. Gorri

Follow C.D. Gorri here:
    http://www.cdgorri.com

https://www.facebook.com/Cdgorribooks
https://www.bookbub.com/authors/c-d-gorri
https://twitter.com/cgor22
https://instagram.com/cdgorri/
https://www.goodreads.com/cdgorri
https://www.tiktok.com/@cdgorriauthor